"The problem is that I get carried away when I touch you,"

Rod told Layne.

A thrill of delight shot through her, followed swiftly by a swell of deep satisfaction. She had a hard time keeping the smile off her face. "I don't mind," she said quietly, hitching up a shoulder.

"Don't you?" he replied doubtfully.

She shook her head. "I know you wouldn't do anything I didn't want you to."

"Not at the moment, maybe," he said gently, "but later it could be very different. Someone has to be sensible, don't you think?"

She bit her lip, knowing he was right, but she didn't want him to be sensible. She wanted him to feel the way she did, though where that might lead she didn't want to contemplate....

Dear Reader,

Summer may be over, but autumn has its own special pleasures—the bright fall foliage and crisp, starry nights. It's the perfect time to curl up with a Silhouette Romance novel.

This month, we continue our FABULOUS FATHERS series with Nick Elliot, the handsome hero of Carla Cassidy's *Pixie Dust*. Under the influence of a little girl's charms and a mother's beauty, even a sworn bachelor can become enchanted by family life.

Love and miracles are alive and well in Duncan, Oklahoma! This little town with a lot of heart is the setting for Arlene James's brand new trilogy, THIS SIDE OF HEAVEN. The series starts off this month with *The Perfect Wedding*—a heartwarming lesson in the healing power of love.

In Elizabeth Krueger's *Dark Prince*, Celia Morawski accepts Jared Dalton's marriage proposal while tangled in the web of her own lies. But is it possible her prince has secrets darker than her own?

Be sure not to miss the fiery words and sizzling passion as rivals fall in love in Marie Ferrarella's *Her Man Friday*. Look for love and laughter in Gayle Kaye's *His Delicate Condition*. And new author Liz Ireland has lots of surprises in store for her heroine—and her readers—in *Man Trap*.

In the months to come, look for more books from some of your favorite authors, including Diana Palmer, Elizabeth August, Suzanne Carey and many more.

Until then, happy reading!

Anne Canadeo
Senior Editor
Silhouette Books

THE PERFECT WEDDING

Arlene James

Silhouette
R O M A N C E™
Published by Silhouette Books New York
America's Publisher of Contemporary Romance

SILHOUETTE BOOKS
300 East 42nd St., New York, N.Y. 10017

THE PERFECT WEDDING

Copyright © 1993 by Deborah A. Rather

All rights reserved. Except for use in any review, the reproduction or utilization of this work in whole or in part in any form by any electronic, mechanical or other means, now known or hereafter invented, including xerography, photocopying and recording, or in any information storage or retrieval system, is forbidden without the permission of the publisher, Silhouette Books, 300 E. 42nd St., New York, N.Y. 10017

ISBN: 0-373-08962-7

First Silhouette Books printing September 1993

All the characters in this book have no existence outside the imagination of the author and have no relation whatsoever to anyone bearing the same name or names. They are not even distantly inspired by any individual known or unknown to the author, and all incidents are pure invention.

®: Trademark used under license and registered in the United States Patent and Trademark Office and in other countries.

Printed in the U.S.A.

Books by Arlene James

Silhouette Romance

City Girl #141
No Easy Conquest #235
Two of a Kind #253
A Meeting of Hearts #327
An Obvious Virtue #384
Now or Never #404
Reason Enough #421
The Right Moves #446
Strange Bedfellows #471
The Private Garden #495
The Boy Next Door #518
Under a Desert Sky #559
A Delicate Balance #578
The Discerning Heart #614
Dream of a Lifetime #661
Finally Home #687
A Perfect Gentleman #705
Family Man #728
A Man of His Word #770
Tough Guy #806
Gold Digger #830
Palace City Prince #866
*The Perfect Wedding #962

*This Side of Heaven trilogy

Silhouette Special Edition

A Rumor of Love #664
Husband in the Making #776

ARLENE JAMES

grew up in Oklahoma and has lived all over the South. In 1976 she married "the most romantic man in the world." The author enjoys traveling with her husband, but writing has always been her chief pastime.

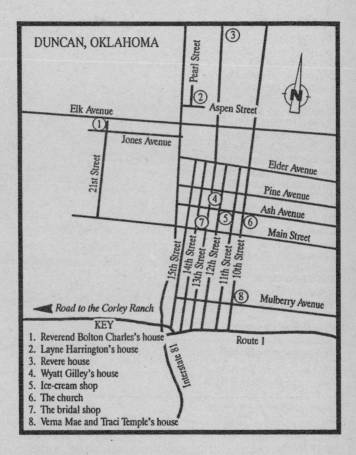

DUNCAN, OKLAHOMA

Pearl Street

Elk Avenue

Jones Avenue

21st Street

Aspen Street

Elder Avenue

Pine Avenue

Ash Avenue

Main Street

15th Street
14th Street
13th Street
12th Street
11th Street
10th Street

Road to the Corley Ranch

Mulberry Avenue

Route 1

Interstate 81

KEY
1. Reverend Bolton Charles's house
2. Layne Harrington's house
3. Revere house
4. Wyatt Gilley's house
5. Ice-cream shop
6. The church
7. The bridal shop
8. Verna Mae and Traci Temple's house

Chapter One

Her business was weddings. Though she did a seasonal business in prom dresses and the occasional evening gown, bridal costumes and the myriad attendant details that occasioned the wearing of them were her stock in trade. And a very good trade it was, too; for in Duncan, Oklahoma, a community of some 25,000 souls or there-abouts, Layne Harington was the one and only full-service wedding consultant. Her skills as a seamstress and designer of exclusive gowns made her stiff competition for any other like-minded business person in the whole of Stephens County. She was it, as far as professional wedding consultation went. Still and all, it was a rare day when a man set foot in her shop, especially a man such as the one who stood before her that September morning.

He was dressed for work in soft, faded jeans, scuffed boots with rounded toes and a white button-down shirt worn so thin by washings and bleachings that the faint, tawny glow of his skin showed through. He held a battered and stained straw cowboy hat in his hands and bowed his head to look at it. Layne saw tiny streaks of gold and silver in his thick sandy brown hair, the former proof that he often worked in the sun without his hat and the latter a testament to his age. He wouldn't see thirty again, that was certain, but when he lifted his head to look at her with smoky, gray-blue eyes bearing only a few shallow lines at the outer corners, she couldn't think him too near forty, either. She smiled and inclined her head.

"Hello, I'm Layne Harington. How can I help you?"

"Ma'am," he said. "I'm told you do weddings—and fine ones at that."

"Weddings are our specialty," she confirmed. "We make all the necessary arrangements and offer a wide variety of choices on everything from invitations to receptions, but it's the customer who makes the decisions."

He nodded and shifted his weight from one foot to the other. "Well," he said, "I'm the customer. Now where do we start?"

Layne tried and evidently failed to control the shock she felt. Men simply did not plan weddings, at least not in her experience. At the most they sat in on the early discussions, grew bored with the many seemingly irrelevant details, then simply left it to the women, reserving only the right to complain about the cost and contest the bills. This man, however, was frowning in a most determined manner.

The frown wrinkled his brow and narrowed his eyes, deepening the lines that fanned out from their corners. His mouth thinned, and his jaw set like concrete. It was surprising, given the intensity of that scowl, that his face remained exceptionally attractive, even handsome. Like the rest of him, his features were large but lean, the skin drawn tautly over prominent cheekbones and a squared chin. His nose was long and straight, his brows golden slashes above deeply set eyes, his mouth wide and finely sculpted with sharp peaks in the center of his upper lip. A lock of sandy brown hair fell over his forehead, golden at the very tip, a single strand of silver shot through it. Yes, a decidedly handsome man. Layne wondered what sort of woman would send a man like this into a shop like hers. Obviously, he could not know what he was letting himself in for. She extended a hand, silently ushering him toward the gracious sitting area where she preferred to stage her consultations.

"What sort of wedding are you interested in?" she asked as they seated themselves on padded wicker chairs situated around a table bearing flowers, a crystal lamp and a number of books and magazines.

He looked out of place and uncomfortable, his hat in his lap. He cleared his throat. "It has to be a proper wedding," he said.

Layne waited for further explanation, but none came. She straightened and smiled sympathetically. "Perhaps we should simply start at the beginning," she said. Reaching down into a box hidden by the tablecloth, she extracted a thin, vinyl-clad notebook embossed with flowers and banded with a strip of paper. A white pen was clipped to the paper band. She broke the band, slipped the pen from it, flipped open the notebook and poised the pen above it. "Your name?"

"Rod Corley."

She began to write in the proper space. "That's *C-o-r-l-y*?"

"*L-e-y.*"

She penned in the final letters. "What size wedding are we talking about, Mr. Corley? How many guests do you expect will attend?"

He shrugged. "I don't know. Quite a few."

She flipped the notebook pages until she came to the one she wanted, then she laid the pen in the fold of the book and turned the book to face him. "I suggest that you begin making a list, Mr. Corley. Take a few days to do it. Be sure to get the bride's input. It need not be complete at this point, but as nearly so as possible. Then we'll simply count, and that will give us a ballpark figure to begin planning with."

He nodded. "All right. What else?"

She sat back and folded her hands, elbows resting on the arms of the chair. "Actually, Mr. Corley, there is a great deal else. Weddings are complicated affairs customarily planned by the bride and her mother."

A spasm of irritation passed over his face. "Does it have to be the bride's mother?"

She lifted her hands in an expansive gesture. "No, of course not. But the bride certainly should be involved."

He nodded and slid his feet back, leaning forward. "Excuse me." Without another word he stood and walked out.

Layne closed her mouth and shook her head. Now she had seen everything. After eight years in this business, which she had started right out of college, she had encountered just about every kind of customer possible, those who knew what they wanted no matter how wild or silly, those who hadn't the vaguest idea, those who could afford just about anything, those who couldn't afford the license, those floating with excitement, those dismayed to the point of tears. But Rod Corley was a first. She didn't have a category in which she could fit him—yet.

Just when she had decided he wasn't going to come back, the chime that signaled the opening of the front door sounded, followed by the muted clump of booted feet on carpet. She swiveled to the side and put on a welcoming smile. Rod Corley stood in the arched doorway of the room, a girl with a baby in her arms at his side. Layne felt the smile dying on her face and quickly bolstered it, coming to her feet. This could not be his bride! She was hardly more than a child herself. Small, waiflike, delicate to the point of frailty. The young mother had a short, neat cap of fine, dark hair that swept in wisps toward a pixieish face overwhelmed by large, dark, frightened eyes. Layne's first reaction was dismay, her second sympathy. She extended her arm in an oddly protective gesture of greeting.

Rod Corley began the introductions. "Miss, or is it Mrs. Harington?"

"Miss."

"Miss Harington, this is Dedrah March."

March. The name was vaguely familiar. Oh, no. She remembered a snippet of gossip she had overheard many months earlier. Before she could check them, her eyes went to the little one perched on Dedrah March's hip. The child gazed back at her with her mother's large, dark eyes, but her hair was both lighter and thicker, very nearly the color of Rod Corley's. Layne felt a sharp sense of disappointment. What kind of man would allow a teenaged girl to bear his child out of wedlock, then show up here wanting to plan a "proper" wedding? It didn't make sense. But it wasn't her job to make sense of such things. She forced the smile back onto her face and decided how she would address the girl.

"Dedrah, I'm Layne. Won't you have a seat?"

The girl nodded and hitched the baby up higher on her hip before crossing to the chair recently vacated by Rod Corley. Layne pulled her own chair around for Rod and another away from the wall for herself, noting that he waited until both women were seated before folding his tall frame into the center chair. Layne pushed the notebook resting on the table closer toward Dedrah. Immediately the baby reached for the ink pen. Dedrah gently pushed her hand away, saying, "No, Heather, you don't need that."

Heather put her hand in her mouth and shrank against her mother, her cheek pressed to the swell of Dedrah's small breast. Dedrah stroked the baby's silky hair and began to rock gently. Layne felt a stab of jealousy. She was at least a decade older than this girl and weddings were her business, but somehow marriage and motherhood had eluded her. She forced her mind to form the necessary question and began.

"Now then, Dedrah, what sort of wedding did you have in mind?"

The girl shrugged. "I don't know."

She certainly didn't sound very excited about the pending marriage, which made this situation all the more unlikely. Layne tried another approach. "Mr. Corley said something about a 'proper' wedding. Does that mean a church wedding with all the trimmings?"

"I suppose," Dedrah mumbled.

Layne glanced at Rod Corley, who nodded. She then took a deep breath. "All right, a church wedding. Did you have a church in mind?"

"No," Dedrah said carefully. "There's this little church in Davis where I used to go, but I suppose that's too far away."

Rod agreed. "Something here in Duncan would be better. I've attended a local church, but it's too small."

"I don't see why," Dedrah said. "My whole family can't add up to more than twenty, and there's just you on the other side."

"There's just me and a couple hundred other people on the other side," he said. "They may not be family, Dedrah, but they're important."

Dedrah sighed and dropped her gaze. Obviously there was some disagreement on the subject. In fact, they seemed to have decided virtually nothing. Layne swallowed the question already on her tongue, reminding herself that their relationship was none of her business, and formed another.

"What date did you have in mind?"

Dedrah looked at Rod, and Rod looked at Layne. "How soon could you get it together?"

Layne pressed both hands against the tabletop as if pressing down her exasperation. "Mr. Corley, I have to know *what* I'm putting together before I can answer that."

He shifted in his seat, irritation flashing across his face again. "Well, figure a couple hundred people," he said flatly, "and a church big enough to hold them."

She decided she was due some irritation of her own. "Two hundred people constitute a fairly large wedding, Mr. Corley," she pointed out. "Will all two hundred be expected at the reception, and what sort of reception are you planning? Will you be serving finger sandwiches or five courses, punch or champagne? Are you expecting out-of-town guests? Will you need special transportation? How many will be in the wedding party? A wedding of that size is usually formal, but how formal depends on a number of things. For instance, will there be a theme? What colors were you thinking of? Have you discussed music, readings, traditions? Who will sing, play, conduct? And what about lighting?"

He held up a hand to silence her. "If I knew what was involved, Miss Harington, I wouldn't be here."

"I'm just trying to give you an idea of what goes into some people's version of a 'proper' wedding."

"All right. Okay," Rod said. "We have to start somewhere. So where would you advise?"

Layne got a grip on herself. "We could start," she said thoughtfully, "with the wedding gown. That would give me some idea of how formal an affair you want and how much money you expect to spend."

"Money's no object," he said quickly, but she had to wonder if he really knew what kind of money they could be talking about. The gown alone could command thousands, but somehow she didn't think that was Dedrah March's style—or Rod Corley's, for that matter.

"Let me show you a few things," she suggested, looking pointedly at Dedrah to let the girl know that she was interested in *her* opinion. The girl nodded, and Corley pushed his chair around to her side, so that both of them faced Layne. She walked to a pair of wide, mirrored doors and opened them to reveal a large room lined with hanging gowns and a spacious freestanding changing booth.

Quickly she went from one rack to another, extracting half a dozen dresses in various styles and price ranges. These she placed on a rolling rack, which she wheeled into the consultation area. There, she took them down one by one and held them out for the couple's inspection, beginning with a simply tailored street-length sheath costing less than two hundred dollars. Rod shook his head sternly at this, and she smiled to herself. Well, it was progress, however slight. The next dress, tea length with a tulip skirt sewn onto a fitted, dropped-waist bodice received the same reception from him, as did the ankle-length princess-style with a demure sweetheart neckline and a sweep train. Dedrah March simply stared, saying nothing, her expression unreadable. When Layne produced the fourth dress, a floor-length traditional gown with a wedding ring collar and fitted bodice trimmed with lace, its full skirt elongated into a court train, Rod Corley nodded with satisfaction.

"That's more like it."

Dedrah glanced down at the little one in her lap, who was mumbling quietly around her fingers. She said nothing about the dress, but her frown indicated displeasure. Layne bit back another inappropriate question, and looked to Rod Corley for guidance. His glance followed her own, and his mouth turned down at the corners. When he once again met her gaze, his irritation was evident, but he nodded for her to go on. Reluctantly, Layne took another dress from the rack and presented it with a flourish.

"This one is a good deal more formal," she said. "The fitted bodice with portrait neckline and Basque waist is appliquéd in lace with seed pearls scattered throughout, as is the hem of the bouffant skirt. The chapel train is separate and extends about four feet from the waist. The cuffs of the Gibson sleeve are four inches long and also appliquéd. The dress runs about twelve hundred dollars, plus alterations."

Both she and Rod looked to Dedrah, whose frown was firmly fixed. Layne rehung the gown and took down the final one. It was considerably more ornate, satin and organza literally encrusted in lace, pearls and frosted sequins. There were bows, some small and others enormous enough to serve as a bustle, a keyhole back, a skirt so full it was both gathered and pleated at the natural waist, leg-of-mutton sleeves, jewel neckline and a detachable cathedral train some three yards in length. At five thousand dollars, it was the most expensive gown in the house. Yet Dedrah's gaze was almost bland.

"It's very pretty," she said, then shook her head. Rod Corley pitched forward in irritation, causing Layne to hastily intercede.

"These are just examples of the different types of gowns," she explained. "There are many, many styles to choose from. If I could just get an idea of what type of dress you're interested in..."

Again Dedrah turned those big, bland eyes up at her and shrugged. Rod Corley smacked his hat against his thigh in frustration, grinding his teeth.

"She won't choose," he said, then, "I knew I should've made Sammy come!"

At that Dedrah clamped her teeth down onto her bottom lip, bowed her head and began to cry. The baby, sensing her mother's distress, squirmed and babbled loudly. Layne realized that soon they would both be in tears, thanks to Rod Corley, if she didn't do something quickly. She shot him a look that told him just who she blamed for the whole situation and watched his mouth drop open, but she had other things to think about at the moment. She threw the dress over the rack, stepped forward and lifted the baby off Dedrah March's lap.

"It's all right," the girl protested, but she said nothing more as Layne thrust the baby at Corley.

"Of course it is," Layne said soothingly, "but perhaps you'd like a drink of water. Why don't you come with me?"

Dedrah nodded and let Layne help her to her feet. Layne ushered the girl through a louvered door set in the corner by the window, down a narrow hallway and through a second door into the workroom, where she pointed out the watercooler. While Dedrah filled a paper cone with water, Layne weighed the wisdom of what she was about to say. It mattered not that it might cost her a customer. She simply didn't want to reduce the girl to tears again, but Dedrah appeared firmly in control now. Layne took a deep breath and folded her arms across her middle.

"Are you sure you want to go through with this?" she asked.

Dedrah looked up in surprise. "The wedding, you mean?" Layne nodded, and Dedrah smiled wistfully. "I do want to get married," the girl said. "I just don't know how it got so complicated."

"I'd say that was Mr. Corley's doing," Layne commented archly.

Dedrah nodded glumly. "Yeah, I suppose it is, but he's such a great guy, you know? He's been really good to us, Heather and me, and he's *so* generous. It's just that he's kind of a take-charge guy, and I guess he's pretty hardheaded, too. Boy, once he's made up his mind to something..." She let the sentence trail off and shook her head. "You know he's just trying to do what's best, but that doesn't always make it any easier. It's just so difficult to tell him to back off once he's got something in his head."

Layne didn't know quite what to make of that description. A great guy, was he? She didn't know if she'd have put that label to him. Generous, maybe, but no doubt the hardheaded part was most apt. "Still," she said, "you shouldn't let him force you into anything."

Dedrah lifted her hands in a gesture of futility. "It's just so complicated," she said softly, "the whole thing, and I suppose it's mostly my fault to begin with. It just seemed so simple once. You're in love, you do what seems natural and too late you realize what a mistake it was. But you live with it, because you love him." She bowed her head, then added hopefully, "We'll work it out."

Layne nodded. She'd embarrassed the girl, and obviously Dedrah had been embarrassed plenty already. Her situation had to be a difficult one, and Layne knew she'd interfered in something that really wasn't any of her business. Enough was enough. She forced herself to relax. "Let's return to the consultation room," she said, "if you're ready."

"Sure. I'm sorry to put you to so much trouble."

"No trouble," Layne replied lightly. "Weddings are very emotional. I'm used to clients who dissolve in tears." It was too true, but Dedrah smiled doubtfully.

"Well, thanks anyway," the girl said, then she tossed her paper cone into the trash can beside the cooler and moved past Layne back the way they'd come.

When they entered the consultation room, giggles greeted them. Dedrah stopped in her tracks and put her hands together, laughing gently. Curious, Layne stepped around her to see what had wrought this transformation. To her surprise, Rod Corley was holding up baby Heather and blowing against her tummy, making the baby giggle and thrash her limbs wildly. Rod dangled her above him, his face wreathed in smiles.

"Whose girl are you?" he cooed, rubbing his face against the baby's. "Whose sweet girl are you? Are you Mommy's girl? Are you Daddy's girl? Or are you Uncle's girl?"

Uncle's? Layne shook her head. Well, he certainly seemed to adore the child. He couldn't be too bad and care that deeply for his baby. She liked him immensely at that moment, and it took all her self-control not to join in the play. She was really a pretty baby and so sweet-tempered. Dedrah was very lucky in many ways.

Once again envy assailed Layne. *One day,* she thought. *It isn't too late. Twenty-nine isn't too old.* She tried not to think that thirty was just around the corner and that it had been years, literally, since she'd had a real date. She tried not to think, too, how often during the early years, when she'd worked so hard to establish her business, her family had warned her that this was going to happen. "You don't want to spend your life alone," her mother had said. "That shop won't kiss you good-night or give you babies." Involuntarily, Layne's eyes went to Rod Corley.

He was pretty long in the tooth for a first marriage, too, but she noticed that he'd chosen a very young woman with whom to begin. She only hoped Dedrah was up to a man as intense as Rod Corley seemed to be, not that any of it was her business. Weddings were her business, and it was time she got back to it.

Layne put an end to the play by walking to the table and picking up the notebook. Behind her, Rod handed over the baby to Dedrah, who immediately took up the cooing.

"You're Mommy's darlin', aren't you? Mommy's sweet, sweet baby."

Layne carried the book to Rod. Evidently he was the one who would be doing the planning, provided any planning was done. "I suggest you take this home and look it over very carefully," she said, "then speak frankly with the bride. If you still want a formal wedding after that, get back to me.''

He stood, and for the first time she realized how very tall he was, a good six inches taller than her five feet and seven inches. He was tall and built like a brick wall, rather imposing taken as a whole, and she took a step backward.

He reached for the notebook as if fearing she would deny it to him, and his hand grazed her wrist. The feeling was sharp and fluid, as if a razor had sliced the skin. She jerked back, releasing the book abruptly, and he grabbed it in midair.

''Ex-excuse me,'' she mumbled, wondering what on earth had gotten into her.

''My fault,'' he replied softly, his aura enveloping her like a cloud, fogging her brain.

''Ah, as I—I said...'' She took a deep, cleansing breath. ''You can get back to me anytime that suits you.''

He nodded and gripped the notebook in long, blunt fingers with very short nails and big knuckles. ''Thank you for your time,'' he said, and his voice sounded oddly deep and bell-like to her ears, as if he had to pull the words up out of the pit of his belly. It made her uneasy. Everything about this man made her uneasy. She managed a smile and turned away, fixing her attention on Dedrah.

''Goodbye. You have a lovely baby.''

''Thanks.'' Dedrah kissed the baby, smiled and walked into the front showroom and out the door, as if she couldn't wait to be shed of the place, while Rod Corley just stood there like a great lump, hat in one hand, notebook in the other, radiating a kind of danger Layne could sense but not identify.

"Mr. Corley," she said, swallowing, "was there something else?"

He looked down at the notebook and up again almost shyly. "You're very nice," he said, adding, "I'm no good when someone cries, and Dedrah's had a pretty tough time of it. I appreciate your kindness."

A strange sensation swept over her, as if a wisp of tulle had brushed the skin all over her body at once. She swallowed convulsively. "I—I understand."

"I thought so," he said quietly. "She's really a timid little thing, too young, but a good mother for all that, and very brave to do it like she has. I want her to have the best."

Layne folded her arms almost defensively. "I see."

"Good." His smile warmed her and dissipated the fog, leaving her with a sense of well-being. "Thanks again." He turned and moved away, but she found she couldn't let him go without speaking her mind.

"Mr. Corley," she called, and he stopped, turning back to face her. Layne licked her lips, then raised her chin. "You'd better have a frank talk with Miss March. You're obviously at odds about this wedding."

He cocked his head as if wondering why she would say such a thing, then looked at the notebook in his hand. "I don't think so," he said, "but we'll talk." He tipped his hat. "So long, Miss Harington."

Layne followed him silently into the front showroom and watched as he opened the door, the chimes pealing, and walked through it. She watched through the glass as he went down the steps and turned onto the sidewalk. He was a good-looking man, but not the type she would have expected to attract or be attracted to the timid, childlike Dedrah. Something wasn't right here, something she couldn't quite put her finger on. She studied his fluid

motions and straight posture as he strode around the
front end of a brand-new pickup truck, climbed into the
cab and settled himself behind the wheel. He spoke to
Dedrah, who was strapping Heather into a car seat between them, but whether the girl replied or not, Layne
couldn't tell. Still speaking, he started the engine, put the
transmission in gear and twisted to spread his long arm
across the back of the seat as he steered the truck out into
the street. Layne turned away from the window before he
started the truck forward and drove away.

They won't come back, she told herself. Dedrah said
he was a good man, trying to do what he thought best.
For some reason, Layne could almost believe that now.
Maybe it was the way he had played with the baby or
what Dedrah had said about being in love, as if that de-
fined her very existence. Rod Corley seemed the sort of
man in whom a woman could lose herself. He would
speak to Dedrah about the wedding, find that she didn't
want to make a production of it and elope. Or maybe
they wouldn't marry at all. Maybe he would look at Dedrah and know that they were a mismatch and such a
mismatch was doomed to failure anyway. He could always be Heather's father without marrying her mother.
Why compound one mistake with another? She shook
her head, trying to derail the train of her thoughts, but it
was a curious thing, a man like that with a girl like that,
when he could probably have his choice of the women
around here.

She remembered the soft warmth of those gray-blue
eyes and the rumbling depth of his voice when he had
thanked her for her kindness, and that curious sensation
swept her again, as if she had somehow been touched
everywhere at once. Yes, a man like that could have almost any woman on whom he set his sights. He didn't

have to seduce innocent young girls. He must love Dedrah with an all-consuming passion that had overwhelmed his better judgment. All-consuming passion? She laughed at herself, glad her two full-time employees were taking an extended break. Outside, a vehicle pulled into a parking space in front of the shop, and Layne welcomed the intrusion into her thoughts. She had work to do. Moving quickly, she rehung the dress she had draped over the portable rack, pushed it into the fitting room, closed the doors and was replacing the chairs at the table when the chimes sounded and a valued customer swept in with her second daughter.

"Mrs. Ogilvy," Layne said, striding forward. "Jennifer. Did we decide on the ribbons?"

"And the shoes!" Mrs. Ogilvy announced proudly, as if they'd made great strides.

Layne suppressed a smile and invited them both to the table. "I'll just get my books," she said, moving toward the desk in the far corner behind the potted ferns.

Only two thousand more details to go, she mused silently.

No, Rod Corley wouldn't be back. He'd take a good look at that planner she'd given him, listen to Dedrah and opt for a simpler process—or no process at all. Either way, she couldn't believe they'd be back. She was almost sorry about that, for she'd like to know what was to become of them. On the other hand, maybe it was for the best. She was entirely too intrigued by that man.

She turned back to Mrs. Ogilvy and Jennifer, offering them her brightest smile. "Well," she said, "let's get down to business." In the end, it was always business for her.

Chapter Two

She was going through a floral design book for the third time with poor, harried Mrs. Stapleton and her petulant daughter, Leslie, when he walked through the door, hat in one hand, notebook in the other, exactly as she'd last seen him some forty-eight hours earlier. The thrill the sight of him brought her was entirely out of proportion with the circumstance, especially since Dedrah March stood beside and slightly behind him, but thrill her he did. She perversely noted that his hair had been carefully parted and combed, that his shirt was fine and crisply pressed, its blue reflected in the starry depth of his eyes, and that his jeans were new and stiff and anchored about his narrow hips with a wide leather belt and palmsize silver buckle bearing the initial C on a bed of black onyx. Moreover, his boots were black and smooth and freshly polished, and the black felt hat in his hand had a narrow brown band sporting a tiny blue-and-yellow feather. Without a doubt, this was Rod Corley turned out in his Sunday best, and if she hadn't known better, Layne would have thought it was for her.

Hastily she tucked that notion into a small, private compartment in her mind and closed the door on it. Rod Corley was here for one reason and one reason only—to plan a wedding, and weddings were her business. She shifted the look of surprise and pleasure on her face, though she couldn't know how much of the latter she had given away in that first unguarded moment. Composed and professional, she excused herself from the Stapleton pair and rose to greet the newcomers with outstretched hands.

"Well, hello."

"Hello."

Rod reached out with both hands, but as his were filled with hat and notebook, she could do little but lay hers gently atop them before quickly taking hers away again. He smiled at her with something very like relief, a reaction she found wholly incongruous. Her cocked head must have said so, for he cleared his throat and injected a businesslike tone to his voice.

"Have we come at a bad time? You did say—"

She cut him off. "No, no, it's fine. If you'll just excuse me a moment, I'll get some help." Smiling benignly, she stepped into the front showroom, where a clerk was ringing up a purchase of lace gloves for a couple of teenagers. "Frankie," Layne said, "could you see to the Stapletons for me?"

The tall, painfully thin Frankie nodded smartly. "Of course."

"Thank you. Call Angie to come up front, please."

"Yes, ma'am."

"And bring coffee for Mrs. Stapleton. Leslie may prefer a soft drink."

"I'll take care of it right away."

Satisfied, Layne turned back to the couple waiting in the arched doorway of the consultation room. "Right this way, please." She led them quickly and swiftly past the Stapletons, who occupied the bamboo table, to the far corner of the room. Screened by a grouping of large ferns in enormous baskets, the area around her desk was suitable for consultation. She used it often when payment was to be made or in the event that two clients were in the shop at the same time for consultation. She indicated two comfortable armchairs standing beside the small, rolltop desk where she did her accounts. Dedrah chose the farthest one, leaving Rod to fold his long frame into the one situated right next to the desk. Layne sat down in the desk chair, swiveled it to face them and crossed her legs. "How may I help you?"

"We're ready to start," Rod said, placing the notebook on the desk and pushing it toward her.

Layne swiveled and opened the cover. Inside she discovered several pages had been filled out in a tight, cramped hand of decidedly masculine origin. She lifted a brow at Rod Corley's anxious expression. "Very good," she muttered, settling back to read. "Let's see what we have here."

Quickly she scanned the pages, some of it written in pencil, some in pen. In the space indicating the chosen date of the ceremony, he had written in pencil, "Soon as possible." The groom was evidently anxious. She bit her lip and went over everything again. He might be anxious to have it done, but he obviously wanted it done right, for the ceremony he had mapped out was both formal and elaborate, and there were more than two hundred names on his guest list. Some of the names were those of Duncan's most prominent citizens, from bank presidents to real-estate agents, oilmen and restaurateurs. It was an impressive list, and she found herself murmuring, "Do you actually *know* all these people?"

"They're my friends," he said blankly, "and business associates. Mostly business associates."

She looked up and smiled, an oblique apology for an insensitive question. "Well, you'll likely add to it as time goes by," she said, then dropped her attention to a second list done in an entirely different hand, Dedrah's no doubt. Less than twenty names comprised Dedrah's list, and nearly all of them ended with March. There was something pathetic about that, and it just pointed out once more how very implausible this match was. It was on the tip of Layne's tongue to say so, and she realized with some panic that she must not. She pushed the book away from her, as if pushing away the words she wanted to say. Her smile was strained when next she lifted her gaze to Rod Corley's, but it was absolutely the best she could do, and she almost hoped it was not good enough. In that case, he would surely get up and walk out, and she wouldn't have to help him marry a woman he shouldn't be marrying. But she was forgetting the child, *his* child, his and Dedrah's. She took a deep breath and reminded herself to remain professional.

"Now I have an idea where we're going," she said briskly. "The next step is to narrow in on a date. Let's see what's going on six to eight months from now." Leaning forward, she began to flip through her personal calendar, speaking to herself. "Let's see, the Cannons are set for April, the Porters are the eighth, the Cliff/Bicknell nuptials on the fourteenth. The Harpstones have the first weekend in May... Oh, dear." She looked up at Dedrah and smiled. "How would you like to be a June bride?" The girl turned white beneath that cap of dark hair.

Suddenly alarmed, Layne leaned forward. "Dedrah, are you all right?"

"June?" Rod Corley's voice claimed Layne's attention. "You've got to be kidding!"

"We can't wait 'til June!" Dedrah gasped.

"Absolutely not," Rod agreed implacably. "Eight months is too long. Six months is too long!"

Layne's mouth fell open. Didn't they understand how much time went into producing the kind of wedding they seemed to want? She slumped, feeling inexplicably weary, then took a deep breath and began carefully choosing her words. "I'm afraid six months is the minimum for the type of ceremony you've indicated here," she said gently. "You can't begin to imagine how much there is to do, how many choices there are to be made. Even the people who come in here confident that they know what they want begin to waffle when they see the available options. It just takes time to work through them all. Weddings are supposed to be perfect, you see, and..." The words died away as Rod Corley passed a hand over his eyes. It was the gesture of a desperate man, and the sight of it did strange things to her patient resolve. She bit her lip. "It takes six months to produce a perfect wedding," she finished lamely.

Rod Corley sighed. "Then we'll have an imperfect wedding," he said quietly, and when he lifted his gaze to her face, his smoky eyes were imploring. "Six months is too long."

Layne found herself saying, "W-we might be able to work something out."

It was then that Dedrah grasped a small part of Rod's sleeve and tugged it, saying, "You'd better get Sammy."

Rod sent her an irritated look and turned back to Layne. "Does it have anything to do with money?" he asked bluntly.

Layne lifted both brows. "Not really. Cash as an incentive never hurts where suppliers are concerned, but the real problem is simply time. It takes time to decide specifics, to make arrangements, to order materials, to create designs..." She shook her head. How could she make him understand the myriads of details to be addressed? "I've been doing this a long time now," she said. "Trust me."

"I do," he told her flatly. "That's why I'm asking you to help me make it happen sooner."

It was not an appeal she could ignore. The tone, the look, the posture, everything about it was totally sincere. He needed her help. It was as simple as that. She swallowed. "I hope you're prepared to spend a lot of time on this," she said.

He reached out and laid his hand over her wrist, squeezing gently. "Thank you," he said, relief softening his voice to a near whisper.

It was almost her undoing. She fought the impulse to cover his hand with her own, to turn soft, hopeful eyes up at him, to flirt shamelessly and pointedly. She edged away from him, breathing deeply and forcing her focus back to business. She made a decision. "Four months," she said, "and that's really pushing it."

"That's the best you can do?"

"The very best, and you're going to have to put yourself completely in my hands at that. We won't have time for second choices."

He nodded. "All right."

To Layne's surprise, Dedrah leapt to her feet. "I'm going after Sammy!" she announced. "You promised him!"

Sammy? Layne looked to Rod for an answer, but he turned his gaze to Dedrah. "I said it'd be done as quickly as possible," he told her patiently, "and that's what I'm doing."

"But four months!" the girl cried.

Rod jerked a thumb in Layne's direction. "You heard what she said," he argued reasonably. "Four months is the best she can do, and I think we ought to be grateful that she's willing to do it for us."

Dedrah glared down at him with very large, very liquid eyes. "You promised Sammy," she whispered.

"So I did," Rod admitted.

"Who—" Layne began, but Rod was suddenly up and striding away. Impulsively, she went after him. "—is Sammy?"

"My nephew," he snapped without slowing a bit.

Layne threw a smile at the Stapletons as she passed. This was impossible. This whole thing with Rod Corley was just impossible, and she made up her mind to tell him so. They hadn't the foggiest idea really what they were doing, and she certainly didn't need this kind of aggravation. Four months was in all likelihood not enough time, and probably after she'd knocked herself out for them, they'd decide they were making a mistake and cancel! Suddenly she didn't know which would be worse, if they canceled or if they didn't. All she really knew was that she didn't feel up to the task of seeing Rod Corley and Dedrah March "properly" married. No, she wasn't going to put herself through this. As soon as they emerged into the front showroom, she lifted a hand to halt his progress, only to watch him stride out of reach and through the door.

"Who," she muttered belligerently, "do you think you are?" She'd just have to tell Dedrah that she didn't want to handle this affair after all. She nodded in satisfaction, then walked to the window and boldly spied on Rod Corley as he stood at the passenger window of the pick-up truck, obviously arguing with someone. After a moment, he backed up, and a tall, lean, young man got out and gestured toward the shop. Both turned in that direction, sending Layne scurrying back into the showroom. Angie, she noticed, sent her a curious glance, which she ignored.

Momentarily, the door opened amidst chimes and Rod Corley stepped inside, the young man at his elbow. "Miss Harington," he said, "this is my nephew, Sammy Corley. Sam, this is Miss Harington. If you won't believe me, then maybe you'll believe an expert." He glanced at Layne. "Tell him."

Tell him what? And why tell him? She opened her mouth and closed it again, forced a smile and said to Sammy, "What is it you'd like to know?"

He pushed a hand through his close-cropped hair, allowing her a few seconds to look him over. The family resemblance was strong, from the color of their hair—though Sammy's was lacking the streaks of silver—to the planes of their faces and the color of their eyes. Sammy was simply a younger, slimmer version of his uncle. Even the timbre of their voices were alike.

Sammy struck a cryptic pose, jerking a thumb at his uncle. "He says it can't be done in less than four months."

He had to be talking about the wedding, of course, but she still didn't understand what he had to do with it. She wondered if she ever would, but nodded and gave him his answer. "Yes. Four months."

"We don't want to wait that long!" he said urgently.

We? Her jaw descended slowly. He couldn't mean he and Dedrah! Could he?

"It's just the best that can be done," Rod was saying. "You understand why, don't you?"

"I understand," Sammy replied, "and we appreciate what you're trying to do, but we don't want to wait."

"I thought you said you wanted it done properly," Rod countered.

"We do!" Sammy said. "We just don't want to wait."

"Well, four months is the best that can be done," Rod said impatiently. "She wanted eight!" He pointed at Layne, who was listening with her mouth hanging open.

"Eight!" Sammy erupted. "No way!"

"Then be grateful she's agreed to do it in four!"

Sammy opened his mouth to make a retort to that, but Layne had had enough. She forestalled him by stepping quickly forward and raising a hand. "Wait a minute!" she commanded, employing a tone usually reserved for the hired help, and Sammy snapped his mouth shut. In the ensuing silence, she tried to decide how to proceed, but there was only one question that really needed answering. She pinned Sammy with a stern look and addressed him. "*Who* are you?" she said, enunciating clearly.

Sammy passed a look to his uncle, who was clearly as befuddled as his nephew. The young man shrugged his shoulders. "Well, I'm—"

"In regard to this wedding," she clarified. "I mean, who are you in regard to this wedding?"

Again, uncle and nephew traded looks, then it was Rod who answered. "Why, he's the groom," he said. "Who'd you think?"

The groom? The *groom!* Layne stepped back and lifted a hand to her mouth. The wave of relief that hit her nearly buckled her knees. "Oh, my," she said, looking at Rod Corley with fresh eyes. A generous uncle. He was nothing more than a generous uncle. This *boy* was going to marry that girl in there. *He* had fathered her child. *Whose sweet girl are you? Are you Mommy's girl? Are you Daddy's girl? Or are you Uncle's girl?* Layne laughed aloud. If that child had any sense at all, she was her uncle's girl and lucky at that. Layne composed herself and offered her hand to Sammy Corley, ignoring the tremor in her voice. "Pleased to meet you," she said, thinking, *Very pleased.* "Miss March is waiting in the next room."

"Thank you," he muttered, then with a speculative look that he shared between them, he slowly turned and started into the consultation room. Layne stood as if rooted to the spot, wondering what to say to the man at her side.

"You didn't really think..."

The sound of his voice prompted her to turn to face him. "What?"

Those smoky blue eyes literally plumbed hers, then he shook his head, a lopsided smile quirking one corner of his lips. "You thought I... and Dedrah...?"

It did seem absurd, always had, and the smile wiggling on her mouth said so, but it was understandable. She dropped her gaze. "What else could I think?"

He chuckled softly, bringing her gaze right back up. Those smoky eyes were as warm as summer skies. "And here I am trying to impress you," he said, his voice low and silky.

She caught her breath. It *was* for her, the new jeans, the blue shirt, the desperately straight part in his sand-and-platinum hair. She was trembling suddenly, as if something momentous had just occurred, something incredible. And hadn't it? No, not yet, but unless she missed her guess it was about to. She was intensely attracted to this man, and he was apparently attracted to her, enough to want to impress her. Was she so wrong to think that something might begin between them if she let him know the attraction was mutual? She hoped not. She surprised herself with how fervently she hoped. She was thinking like a schoolgirl, but she wasn't about to act like one.

She straightened her spine and lifted her chin, adopting her best business tone. "Try no more," she said. "I was impressed to begin with." She strode forward, reveling in the rich laughter that followed her.

It was that laughter, augmented with smiles, that bolstered her during what was to be a difficult consultation, for if Dedrah was uncertain, her intended was not. He didn't want this wedding. He didn't say so in words, but he didn't have to; Layne had become adept over the years at reading the silent body language of her clients. A stony face, and she had seldom seen one stonier, was a sure sign of dislike. When she added a fist that reflexively clenched then deliberately relaxed, a leg that jiggled uncontrollably and a frown that turned too quickly to a lusterless smile, she came up with a fellow trying to appear accepting of something he did not truly want.

The question was why he was playing the game, for Dedrah's sake or for Rod's? The latter seemed unlikely. Sam could save his uncle a bundle by expressing a preference for a simple service, so he had to be keeping quiet for Dedrah's sake. He wouldn't be the first groom to indulge his bride, and yet something about this whole arrangement didn't quite add up. Rod had said he wanted Dedrah to have the best, and apparently Sammy did, too, so why wasn't Dedrah enthusiastically embracing everything Layne had to offer? Maybe the girl just didn't know what she wanted. Maybe she didn't know what a "proper" wedding actually entailed, and maybe she felt guilty about the amount of money Rod would have to spend in order to provide her with one. Whatever the problem, Layne concentrated on making Dedrah feel relaxed and included, while actually leaving her very few decisions. Time dictated the leeway Layne could allow in this case, and everyone seemed to accept her "suggestions" until they came to the matter of guest lists again.

"I think we should plan for no fewer than three hundred guests," Layne contended. "Dedrah, you're bound to think of a few names you'll want to add to your list before the invitations go out, and both sets of parents will likely want their friends included."

"I don't think so," Dedrah replied in a small voice.

At the same moment Sammy shook his head. "Me, neither. Till we're married, Rod's all I've got in the way of family."

Layne could not prevent her gaze going up to Rod's face. He was leaning against the wall, arms folded, the toe of one boot hooked around the heel of the other. Those smoky eyes were trained on Layne's face, and she had the distinct impression that they had been there all along. Despite the little thrill that swept through her, she forced herself back to business.

"I know you think that now," she told the pair confidently, "but experience tells me that you *will* add to the list. Don't worry, we'll eventually cut back, but the time for that is after the RSVP's come in. I'm guessing we'll wind up around two hundred and fifty, but in the meantime we plan for three hundred. That leaves us a comfortable cushion. It also means that any surprises at the end will be pleasant ones in terms of expense. Now, are we agreed here?''

"We're agreed," Rod said flatly. After a hesitation, during which he reached over and clasped Dedrah's hand, Sammy nodded his acquiescence. Only then did Dedrah give hers. Layne breathed a silent sigh of relief. The matter was settled, and Sammy did seem to be holding back for Dedrah's sake. However, if Rod Corley had his way, no one would be holding back for very long. He was an amazingly generous man, and family seemed to mean a great deal to him. She smiled to herself, remembering the way he'd cooed to Sam's and Dedrah's baby. "*Are you Uncle's girl?*" A man like that should have had babies of his own. She wondered why he hadn't, then wondered if maybe he had. But no, a family of Rod's would have been family of Sammy's, and Sammy had made it plain that he had only Rod—for now. When Sammy married, both he and Rod would expand their family. Maybe that explained Rod's generosity. "I want her to have the best," he had said of Dedrah. Yes, family meant a lot to Rod Corley. Layne was impressed, but again she made herself turn her thoughts to business. Producing a wedding of this magnitude in only four months time left no room for dillydallying.

"Location," she said. "I'll call around to those local churches that can accommodate a wedding of this size and find out which ones have open dates about four months from now. Let's schedule another meeting. Oh..." She flipped through her calendar again. "How's Friday?''

"Fine," Rod said, and nobody else bothered to argue.

"About four-thirty?"

"We'll be here."

Not *they* but *we*. Because of her? Layne wondered. Did he want to see her again, or was he just that rare man who actually enjoyed planning weddings? She smiled to herself as Dedrah and Sammy got to their feet, then quickly composed herself and rose also.

"We'll see you, Miss Harington," Sammy said, his hand resting in the small of Dedrah's back.

"You're kind to do this for us in so short a time," Dedrah added, but Sammy snorted.

"Four months looks like four years just now, if you ask me."

"Well, nobody did," Rod said, a hand falling on Sammy's shoulder. "Now scoot. I need a word with Miss Harington."

Layne took pains to smile at Dedrah. "I look forward to seeing you again. Good day."

"So long, ma'am." Dedrah and Sam turned and left them, their arms linked about one another's waists.

Layne stood beside Rod and looked up at him. "Walk me out?"

"My pleasure," she said, and he gave her a smile that warmed her from the inside out.

"I, um, just wanted to thank you again," he said, "and, ah, explain about Sam."

She cocked her head to one side. "What about him?"

He reached out a hand and cupped her elbow, turning her smoothly, and they began to stroll after Sam and Dedrah. "Actually, it's about Heather," he said haltingly. "Sammy didn't know Dedrah was pregnant when he went to Saudi Arabia."

"He's military, then?" That explained the haircut.

"Was. He just got out. If I'd had my way, he'd never have enlisted, but it was done by the time I found out about it. Anyway, apparently they had some kind of fight—and that's another thing. I didn't even know they were seeing one another. I mean, I knew he was going out when he was home on leave, but I didn't know who with. I figured he was seeing lots of girls, but instead he was seeing just one, and obviously things got pretty serious. But then they had this fight, and they broke up. I don't think he was very happy about it, because he did write her from Saudi Arabia. I guess she had her reasons for not telling him about the baby."

"I can understand that," Layne said quietly. They had walked past Frankie and the Stapletons, and she was anxious to keep the conversation private, considering the delicate nature of the subject. That being the case, she stopped right beneath the arch that led out into the front showroom, keeping as much distance as possible between the two of them and the Stapletons with Frankie on one hand and Angie on the other. "I would imagine Dedrah didn't want him to feel pressured," she said. "They had broken up. He had gone off to war. It wasn't as if he could do anything about it from Saudi Arabia."

"No, it wasn't," Rod agreed, "especially as he didn't know. But like I said, I think he cared about her all along, because when he got stationed over at Ft. Sill, he didn't waste any time looking her up, and apparently as soon as he laid eyes on Heather he knew she was his."

"And naturally he claimed her."

"Not yet," Rod said uneasily. "I mean, not legally. The wedding will pretty much take care of that, but we haven't figured out exactly how to handle the rest of it. The wedding's the important thing, though. If we do that right, that's half the battle. It took him some time to convince Dedrah that he really wanted to marry her." Rod went on. "He was back in this area a couple of weeks before I even found out any of this."

"And when you did, you offered them the wedding of their dreams," Layne supplied helpfully.

Rod grinned. "Something like that. The point is, Sam's a good kid who's made a mistake, and now I'm trying to help him overcome it, not that any of us consider Heather a mistake, mind you. It's just that they did kind of get the cart before the horse, and now they've got to...well, hold their heads up and fix it. They're doing the right thing by getting married, but I personally think *how* they do it is important, too. I mean, if they slink off and do it in some shabby little office somewhere, that's the same as saying they're ashamed, don't you think?"

Layne shrugged uncomfortably. This really wasn't any of her business, but he had asked. "I don't know. I suppose some people might think so."

"Right, and I just don't see why those kids ought to have to deal with that. Besides, they have every right to a fancy wedding. You understand what I'm saying?"

"I think I do," Layne said. "You don't want them to miss out on anything."

"Them or that little girl," he said, then a pained expression flitted across his face. "I know this wedding's liable to cause some gossip," he went on, "and God knows Dedrah's had plenty of that already. If people only knew when they started whispering tales how much hurt they were causing, there wouldn't be any such thing as gossip, but nobody seems to consider that, and I've no reason to think they will now. But I think it'll all turn out for the best if we just keep our heads up and go on as we would have if they hadn't made that one mistake."

Layne smiled and was bold enough to reach out and squeeze his shoulder. "I think they're very lucky to have you," she told him.

His head bowed, and he started working his way around the brim of his hat with both hands. She took her hand away, and he said softly, "I think we're all very lucky to have found you to help us," he said.

Layne put her head back and laughed. "Mr. Corley," she said, "you could hardly have missed me. In case you haven't noticed, I'm the only game in town."

"And most any other woman in that position would be a real snooty sort," he said, "but you're not like that at all."

She actually felt herself blush. "That's very kind of you to say."

"Kindness deserves kindness," he said softly, and for just a moment Layne had the crazy notion that they were somehow set apart from the others in the building. She could see and hear the others around them, and yet the spot where they stood had the most amazingly intimate aura about it. She had that curious sensation again of being touched all over at once by some unseen, feather-light hand, and she shivered from the delicious feel of it. That was when everything snapped back into perspective, and she saw clearly that they enjoyed no privacy whatsoever.

She lifted her chin, swallowed and wrapped her arms about herself as casually as she could manage. "You know, you really don't owe me any explanations," she pointed out. "I'm hired help, and because my services aren't free, it pays to be on my best behavior with all my clients. If some are easier to be kind to than others, well, that's a blessing."

"I just thought it'd help if you understood the circumstances fully," he said, and she nodded.

"It does. Thank you."

"You're welcome. Now would you do me a favor?" he asked, his voice husky and low.

Anything, she thought, but wisely she said only, "If I can."

He lifted his hat and fitted it carefully onto his head, saying, "Now don't agree too fast. This is a biggie."

Somehow she doubted it. The gleam in his smoky blue eyes seemed to say that he was teasing. "What?" she urged, her face perfectly blank.

He tugged his hat brim down over his eyebrows and leaned forward, whispering, "Call me Rod."

The corners of her mouth quirked upward. "My name is Layne, in case you've forgotten," she said, and those blue-gray eyes twinkled brightly.

"I haven't forgotten."

She nodded, feeling terribly conspicuous where moments before she'd felt set apart, and said, "See you Friday, Rod."

He shot her a smile like white lightning. "I'll be looking forward to it. Layne."

He tipped his hat and left her. Her heart was beating a slow, steady, but very pronounced staccato. *Not the groom at all,* she thought. *And people say there isn't a God.* She smiled to herself. Only four months, but this was going to be a wedding to really make Rod Corley proud. It was going to take lots of her personal attention, she decided, more so than any wedding she'd ever handled. But something told her it was going to be worth it. Cherishing that secret, she turned back to Mrs. Stapleton and Leslie, and this time her smile was the real thing. Never mind that it wasn't for them.

Chapter Three

Layne had plenty of time to talk herself into a state of tranquillity before Friday, and yet, by the time that last appointment of the day drew near, she was painfully conscious of a fluttering in her stomach. It was not unlike that moment when all her efforts seemed to culminate: the church was filled, the music ceased, the mother of the bride and both of the groom's parents were seated, the wedding party in all its finery poised on the brink of movement, and then began the processional. Step, pause, step. Step, pause, step. Maids in beautiful dresses, their faces composed with serenity and joy, moved down the aisle on the arms of tuxedoed young men, grave and solicitous. Then came "The Wedding March," those first familiar notes ringing out with the authority of trumpet blows, and the crowd rose expectantly to its feet. Posed in the doorway was the bride in all her elegant finery, clutching the arm of a nervous father. She was always extraordinarily beautiful, and it never failed to thrill

Layne that all the old pundits were right. The groom took one look and his chest swelled with pride, his eyes sparkled, and a smile touched his lips.

This was love, the very height of it, when commitment was made and reveled in. Everything after that moment was anticlimactic to Layne, though she knew it was not so for the couple involved. For them, the pageant had only begun, while her part in it was all but finished. Sometimes she wondered if she didn't stay in this business just for the satisfaction of that one moment when she recognized love rewarded in the eyes of the groom as he saw his bride as the most beautiful creature on earth. Just once she wanted a groom's eyes on her.

It was the foolish thought of a natural-born romantic, and she thrust it away as soon as it formed, but it came flooding back to her when she heard chimes and turned to find Rod Corley staring at her, an appreciative gleam in the dusky blue depths of his eyes. Immediately the butterflies in her stomach took flight, shivering throughout her body, and she was immensely grateful that she had dressed that morning with particular care. She rejected the impulse to smooth the deep coral bouclé knit of her slim skirt and tug at the ribbed hem of the soft matching sweater. Instead, confident that the color of the suit picked up the auburn highlights in her nut-brown hair while its soft, slender shape made the most of her figure, she brought her hands together and smiled.

Heather was riding high in the crook of his arm, one chubby fist grasping his ear. Sammy and Dedrah stood at his back. The off-white sweater he wore with his jeans and boots made his hair seem darker by contrast and more of a single color. His hat was in his free hand.

"Hello."

Just the sound of his voice warmed her almost uncomfortably, and she had the odd sensation that she was swaying dizzily; yet her mind was clear, her senses sharp. She let her eyes meet his and made her smile briefly personal. "Hello."

"Hope you don't mind that we brought Heather along again, but I thought it important that we all be here, and Dedrah's mother had a doctor's appointment. We don't much like to leave her with anyone else. She's used to her grandma."

We? She wondered if he realized how much he revealed about his feelings for that child. "No, I don't mind at all."

"I didn't think you would. Besides, she's no trouble." He turned his attention to the baby. "You're no trouble, are you, sweetcakes?"

In reply, the little one put her arms about his head and squeezed, planting a sloppy kiss on his forehead. Everyone laughed, and Heather gave them a drooling smile, then suddenly began climbing over Rod's shoulder to reach for her father. Sammy swung her down and settled her on his hip, while Dedrah chased the drools back up her little chin with a tissue.

"No!" Heather said, throwing back her head. "No—no."

"Yes," Dedrah reprimanded quietly, wiping her chin dry.

Rebelliously, Heather lunged for "Uncle," catching her tiny hands in his sweater. Calmly, he turned and took her up again, saying, "Are you trying to make a liar out of me, shorty?" With perfect comic timing, she nodded emphatically, and everyone laughed again. "Well, you're succeeding," Rod told her, the very picture of patience.

Layne decided it was time to get everyone settled. She lifted an arm invitingly. "I have coffee and soft drinks in the other room, and I think I can find a can of fruit juice for the munchkin."

"That's all right," Dedrah said, extracting a bottle from her purse. "We came prepared."

Heather promptly snatched the bottle from her mother's hand and popped the nipple in her mouth. Rod rocked her back in his arm, cuddling her against him, and she crossed one little ankle over the other little knee, looking for all the world as if she were kicking back on a chaise longue. Amazing, the way he handled her. Layne started toward the consultation area, and Rod fell in at her side, the others following.

"I'll get another chair," she said, skirting the table and heading toward the workroom.

"Let me help," he insisted, tossing his hat onto the table, and though she opened her mouth to tell him not to bother, she found herself smiling instead of talking. Heather in tow, he followed her down the corridor to that place where she felt most at home, the workroom, the creative heart of her whole operation. It was here that every young woman's dream gown was "sculpted" to fit her personal form or, better yet, designed and sewn especially for her, a true one-of-a-kind garment.

Layne knew all too well that she was very small potatoes indeed compared to the world-famous couturiers of New York, London or Rome, but she still took pride in her designs and special adaptations. Ethics forbade her "knocking off" another's dress, but she had found over the years that she could take a basic pattern or a significant feature and build a garment around it that was both unique and pleasing to the client. It was very satisfying to see the joy in the eyes of a happy bride when her own special wedding gown met her hopeful expectations. There were disappointments, of course, such as clients who couldn't be pleased or didn't know their own minds, but one of the other kind was worth two such as these, and so Layne counted herself lucky to be doing what she did. Some of that pride must have communicated itself to Rod, for he took one look around the room when they got there and lifted his free hand to the back of his neck.

"Wow. I didn't know. I mean, I thought you only *sold* dresses and bows and stuff." He walked over to a fitting double and looked at the unfinished dress pinned to the carefully measured contours of the adjustable mannequin. "You start from scratch, don't you?"

"Sometimes."

"What do you begin with? A bolt of material and..."

"An idea," she said. "It always starts with an idea." She went to the drawing table and carefully peeled up a large sheet of paper.

Rod joined her, holding Heather to one side so that her tiny feet had no opportunity to kick at the drawing, and peered down over Layne's shoulder to study the detailed rendition of an elaborate gown of medieval design. She heard the slow intake of his breath and the low whistle that followed it. He turned his head to look again at the mannequin. "Is that this?"

"No. We haven't cut this one yet. That dress goes with the drawing pinned to the bulletin board over there."

He strolled over to take a look, capturing Heather's little hand in time to prevent her ripping down a bright pink invoice of some sort. He studied the drawing that hung beside it, then backed away, shaking his head. "You're a woman of extraordinary talents, Layne," he said, turning a look of more than mere approval upon her.

"Thank you." She felt as if she were glowing. Her heart was tripping like a jackhammer in double-time, and the pleasure was almost too wonderful to bear. She dropped her head and angled it to the side, spying the chair for which they'd come. At the same moment, Heather popped the bottle nipple out of her mouth and filled the room with a soft gurgling sound, lending a touch of her own brand of baby normalcy to the situation. "We ought to get back," Layne said with a smile.

"Oh, right. Is that the chair you want, the folding one?"

"Yes, but as you see, it's very light. I can get it."

"No, no. I'll manage."

Their hands collided against the smooth, cool metal of the chair back. Her immediate impulse was to withdraw, but his hand settled warmly over hers, his palm replacing the two smallest fingers that had initially made contact. Warmth spread up her arm and into her chest. Her heart swelled to the point of pain. For a moment she could neither speak nor breathe, but she looked away and the moment passed.

"This is silly," she said, willing her hand to remain still beneath his. "You have the baby. I should carry the chair."

"Or..." he suggested, and her gaze zipped up to the baby cradled in the crook of his arm.

Her own eagerness surprised and amused her. Sensing that she was suddenly the center of attention again, Heather snapped her bottle free and gave off a broad, wet smile that displayed all ten of her tiny teeth. Rod chuckled and wiped her mouth with the flat of his hand, drying his hand on his pants leg.

"She might get apple juice on that pretty outfit of yours," he said.

Layne didn't even bother to tell him how little that mattered. Instead, she asked, "Do you think she'd let me hold her?" Heather stuck the nipple back in her mouth and drew on it strongly.

"This kid is so secure," Rod said, smoothing down her hair, "that she isn't afraid of anyone, and we can credit her mama with that." Suddenly Heather decided to change positions. Her bottle dangling from her mouth, she used her little hands to claw her way upright. Laughing, Rod allowed her momentum to carry her into Layne's waiting arms.

The baby was surprisingly heavy, but it was love at first cuddle. "Hi, peach," Layne said softly, using her father's pet name for all three of his daughters. Heather dug a chubby finger into the center of a tiny crocheted flower on the tip of Layne's collar. "You like my rose?" Layne crooned. "Pretty rose."

To her surprise, Heather reached up a hand to unplug the bottle from her mouth and said, "Roe."

Layne laughed with delight. Rod grinned, folding up the chair. "Another day, another conquest," he said, sighing. "Must be nice to have all that charm."

"As if you didn't know!" she retorted unthinkingly.

He straightened with the chair, a look of surprise on his face. Then his eyes went to hers and probed deeply. She hadn't known they could be so blue! They seemed to withdraw by increments until he was looking at the section of the back of the chair between his two hands. "No one's ever even hinted that I might be charming before," he said quietly.

She didn't know what to say to that. "I . . . It seemed so—"

Heather decided it was time to get back to her parents. "Ma-ma!" she called loudly.

"Obvious," Layne finished.

Rod laughed. "What's obvious here is that we've been gone too long. Come on, ladies. Time to talk weddings."

Layne didn't know if she was relieved or disappointed, but she followed along, whispering baby talk to Heather, who now seemed intent on plucking the "roe" from Layne's collar. As soon as they appeared in the consultation room, Sammy jumped up and came forward to take the baby. Layne gave her over wistfully and reached for her chair, but Rod had already beat her to it, having set the folding chair for himself. It was such a mundane courtesy, and yet she felt her color heighten as she lowered herself into the chair that Rod held for her. As usual, she took refuge in professionalism.

"Now, then, who has the notebook?" she asked.

"Oh," said Dedrah, "I do." She picked up her purse and extracted the notebook from it, placing it on the table.

Layne pulled it over and opened it. As she had suspected, Rod had added several names to his list, but Dedrah had added none, and neither, Layne suspected, had Sammy. She considered asking why, then decided against it. Despite her growing familiarity with Rod, who Dedrah and Sammy invited to their wedding was really none of her business. She made herself move on to other things.

"Let's get the wording of the invitations out of the way," she decided briskly. She reached for a large book that included samples of stationery, print type and composition. Quickly she went over only the most formal sorts; as she did so, she noted idly that Sammy wasn't paying the least attention. Instead, he played with Heather, giving her a "horsey" ride on his knee. Rod, on the other hand, pulled his chair close and leaned forward, his shoulder overlapping hers.

"I think I like this one," he said after a bit, pointing out a very formal embossed card. "Of course, we can't use the traditional wording because both of Sammy's parents are deceased."

"We could put your name there," Layne told him. "It certainly seems appropriate."

"I guess," he mused, "but I don't see that it's needed. Why can't they just invite people to their own wedding?"

"They can. How about something like this?" She pointed to another sample.

"Hmm, simpler seems more classy to me."

"All right, let's see what we can come up with ourselves." She pulled forward a notepad and pen and began writing. After a few moments, Rod took the pen from her and scribbled words of his own. She pointed out a problem, and he scratched through his composition to start over. She didn't realize how completely they'd shut out the bride and groom until she heard giggling and looked over to find Dedrah's chair empty. Puzzled, she craned forward and scanned the area, finding both Dedrah and Sammy on the floor with Heather, playing a hands-and-knees version of chase. She looked at Rod, who merely smiled and went back to penning his version of the wedding invitation. Layne bit her lip, but again stifled the urge to speak out. Instead, she got up and announced that it was time to look at dresses again. Surely Dedrah would participate in choosing her own wedding gown.

As before, Layne went into the fitting room and chose several samples of formal dresses. When she wheeled them out into the consultation area, Sammy reluctantly picked up Heather and carried her back to his chair. Dedrah sat glumly and simply watched, while Rod hitched his chair around and eagerly anticipated the first viewing.

Layne went through her repertoire, babbling on and on about bodices and sleeves, waistlines and necklines, skirt types and fabrics and a myriad of decorations and embellishments. All the while, Dedrah's elfin face remained impassive and Sammy entertained the baby. It became painfully obvious that Layne was playing to an audience of one, and that one was Rod, who looked gradually more and more puzzled as Dedrah and Sammy detached. Finally he got up and walked over to Layne.

"Do you have anything in her size?" he whispered. "Maybe if she could try some on, something would hit her."

"Good thinking." Layne turned to Dedrah. "I'm guessing you're a size three."

"Mmm-hmm, but I can wear a five in some things."

"All right. How about if I get together all my threes and a few fives and you can try them on?"

Dedrah grimaced. "I don't have the right underthings with me. Maybe we should wait."

Layne sent a silent plea for assistance to Rod. He furrowed his brow, then brightened. "I know, Layne can model for us."

It was something she'd done fairly often, actually, and something she enjoyed. Plus, she could involve Dedrah by asking her to help with the changing. To her relief, Dedrah agreed readily, and they closed themselves into the fitting room to pick the gowns Layne would model. When she emerged in the first one, a simple empire style with draped neckline and sleeves, even Sammy gave her his attention. By the third gown, which featured a tulip skirt, petal sleeves and a cameo neckline, both Rod and Sammy were offering comments.

"I liked the last one better."

"That's neat, the way the skirt folds there."

"What'd you call that thing in the back, a butterfly?"

At about the fourth dress, which had a fitted bodice with a portrait neckline, dropped waist and long sleeves over a soft, full skirt, Sammy said, "I can see you in that one, Dee. That's the first one that really looks like you."

But it was the fifth and Layne's favorite gown that brought Rod slowly to his feet. Pleasure suffused her as she posed for his perusal. His eyes smoky with gray again, mouth slightly ajar, he walked around her in a wide arc, halting only at the edges of the cathedral train that swept across the floor behind her. The strapless ball gown was constructed of silk Charmeuse and venise lace. The waistline dropped into a V at the base of the spine, with the train attached in gathers so tight, they formed opulent folds caught into a low bustle. Over her bare shoulders she wore a short brocade jacket encrusted in beads and pearls and sporting a modified Queen Anne neckline and cap sleeves. She had also donned the long, matching gloves appliquéd with bits of lace and cuffed just above the elbows with encrusted brocade. Even without the tiara and cathedral-length organza veil, this costume solemnly proclaimed itself fit for royalty.

"I've never seen anything like it in my life," Rod said huskily. "Your own design?"

"Yes."

He nodded. "It looks like it was made just for you."

She cast down her gaze nervously. "I suppose in a way it was."

"Wouldn't you mind if someone else wore it?" he asked gently.

Her gaze slid up again. How had he known? Since the day she'd conceived the gown, she'd held a secret vision of herself gliding down the aisle in it. The complete dress had been jealously guarded, shown only to a select few as an example of her work and priced well beyond the means of all but the wealthiest of her clients. She had modeled it today for one reason, to show off in front of Rod Corley. Never in her wildest imaginings had she dreamed he would react with such tender appreciation, such *wonder*. She turned away as best she could, the gown swishing heavily about her legs, and managed to say in a level tone, "No one ever has. I suppose it's a little too . . . specialized."

He reached out as if to touch her sleeve, then abruptly withdrew. "No one ever should—but you." He cleared his throat. "It wouldn't suit Dedrah anyway. I, um, think we should concentrate on . . . a more tailored style."

Sam spoke up then. "All that fussy stuff is too overpowering for Dee. She's too little for it."

"You're quite right," Layne agreed, relieved to be talking business again. "I'll get out of this and see what I can find in her size similar to that last dress. Will you help me, Dedrah?"

Backing into the fitting room was easier than turning around with nine feet of train and twenty yards of skirt trailing after, and once behind closed doors, it took some time to get out of the dress. While Dedrah worked to set her free, Layne's mind was going over every likely dress in the shop, busily matching each with Dedrah's fragile size and slight stature. Suddenly she knew what would work. It was only a bridesmaid's design, but the more she thought of it, the more she knew it would work, especially if they narrowed the skirt and added a bustle and train. As she quickly donned her own clothing again, she was sketching in her mind, "building" Dedrah the perfect dress. When she was through, she had mentally designed a dropped waist bodice that buttoned up the front, had long, slender sleeves and a Queen Elizabeth portrait collar, closing in an inverted V in front. The skirt would be especially graceful, softly gathered in front to create an almost smooth horizontal panel and fully gathered in the back to add a more voluptuous shape, with a bustle constructed of a single pouf and a cathedral-length train suitable for a formal ceremony. They would use silk-faced satin and embroidered brocade, with only a touch of lace at the hem of the skirt and sleeves and along the edges of the train. The headpiece would be a Juliet cap covered in brocade and topped with a swirl of net. It would carry three simple layers of veiling, the first falling just below the chin, the second at the shoulders and the third trailing to chapel-length.

Excitedly, Layne pulled down the dress upon which she intended to base her design and almost bullied Dedrah into it. Then, with pins and a few scraps of fabric from the dress already under construction in the workroom, she created the necessary illusions. Finally, using parts of two different veils and a poorly fitting Juliet cap, she fashioned a facsimile of the headpiece she had in mind and backed up to take a good look. Yes. It was perfect. Dedrah, who had gotten a running commentary the whole time Layne was preparing the costume, actually seemed enthusiastic, though uncertain about the fabrics Layne suggested for the actual garment. Still, the big test was ahead of them. Hopeful, Layne opened the door to the fitting room and led Dedrah out for viewing.

"Gentlemen," she said, "what do you think?"

Sammy cocked his head, seemingly indifferent, but Rod frowned consideringly at the rose pink shade. "Shouldn't it be white?" he asked.

Layne smiled, understanding completely his dissatisfaction. "Yes, but not stark white, something softer like candlelight or blush white. Because of her delicate skin coloring and dark hair, a stark white would be unflattering. I also suggest we forgo the traditional use of lace, except for edgings, and concentrate on opulent fabrics such as silk-faced satin and a particular embroidered brocade. I have a sample over here."

She motioned Rod to follow her and strode toward the table. Selecting a book, she flipped through it until she found what she wanted. It was a soft, glowing white with a bluish tint, brocaded and embroidered in a shade known as candlelight which, compared to the background, was almost a pale yellow. She ripped the sample out of the book and positioned it over a black background to emphasize its whiteness. Rod studied it, then smiled.

"This is for the top part of the dress, right?"

She could have kissed him. "Exactly! Except the collar. The collar and the skirt will be satin, edged with tiny but heavy lace. Crocheted maybe. What do you think?"

He turned to take another look at Dedrah. "Do you like it?" he asked the girl.

She nodded. "Yeah. Yeah, I like it."

Rod lifted a hand to the back of his neck, turned, then smiled at Layne. "Let's do it," he said. "You want a deposit so you can order the material?"

She laughed brightly, feeling as if she'd made a wonderful coup. "Give me a day or two to get the design on paper and figure how much we'll be needing. Then I'll give you a call, and you can bring in a deposit. All right?"

"Fine. You have my number, don't you?"

"Yes, and mine is on the front of the notebook I gave you." She had a sudden thought and hastily added, "The shop number, I mean. I'll, ah, write my home number below it. That way, you can call me anytime you have a question." Busily, she reached for the notebook, closed it, and penned her home number on the cover. Her hand was shaking. It was unforgivably bold of her. She never gave out her home phone number. If she did, she'd be pestered day and night by jittery clients, but he couldn't know that. Besides, it was a legitimate exception to the rule. They were trying to produce a formal wedding in a ridiculously short time. *And it has nothing whatsoever to do with the fact that you nearly melt and run all over his feet every time he looks at you, right?* Wrong. She was never any good at lying to herself. Maybe she would be better at it with him. She closed the book and handed it to him. "Next time you come I'll have a place and time in mind, so we can finish writing the invitations. Oh, and I need your permission to place an announcement in the newspaper."

"Is that necessary?" The voice was Sammy's. Dedrah had gone to change back into her street clothes. Rod turned and stepped aside so that she had an unobstructed view of Sam, who rose to his feet and swung Heather up to his hip. He lowered his voice. "People will ask questions. I don't want people coming up to Dee and asking all kinds of unnecessary personal questions." He looked pointedly at Heather, then smoothed down the child's fine hair as if apologizing for some unwelcome thought. Layne felt certain she knew what that thought was. Dedrah had almost certainly suffered a great deal.

An unmarried woman having a child alone was not the pariah society once would have made her, but she was still the object of much gossip and conjecture. This wedding would undoubtedly revive much of the old pain, and the wounds could not yet be totally healed. So far, everything they'd done had been private and easily undone, but a public notice of engagement would be very nearly irrevocable. Even a broken engagement could not be announced as publicly.

"A newspaper announcement is traditional," she said, "but not necessary."

"I disagree."

She turned a surprised look at Rod, who was frowning very deeply. "No, really," she said, thinking he did not understand. "People do primarily what they want to. Many still do choose to observe the traditional conventions, but it's not *necessary*."

"I think it is." His voice was unusually deep and edged with steel. "In this case, any lapse in the 'traditional conventions,' as you put it, would be like an admission of shame, and that's the last thing Dedrah or Sammy need."

"The only one who's ashamed is me," Sammy said defensively. "I got her pregnant and then I left her alone to deal with it. I should've known that could happen, but I didn't even think about it. I should've been here to protect her, but I wasn't. Well, I am now, and I'm telling you she's been through enough. Informing friends and family is one thing. Announcing it to the general public is something else."

"Everyone's going to know anyway," Rod argued. "It's better to make the announcement and just face down the gossips."

"Better for you and me," Sam said, "but not for De-drah. You don't know her like I do, Rod. She's not as strong as she seems."

"I think you're wrong."

"I'm not backing down on this," Sam said stubbornly. "I mean it."

Rod scowled, and Layne held her breath. What was it about him that made him seem so fierce? One moment he was all tender smiles and glowing eyes, and the next he was authority itself, implacable, impregnable. She had no doubt that if he decided to fight he would win, and Sammy must have known it, too. Yet, the younger man stood his ground, chin high, gaze level. After a long, tense moment, Rod nodded and gruffly conceded. "All right, if that's the way you want it."

Sammy looked almost sheepish in his relief, but said only, "Thanks," before settling his attention on the baby once more.

Layne smiled and pulled a tremulous breath. She didn't relish the idea of refereeing any argument in which Rod Corley participated, particularly when she agreed with his opposition. Thank goodness he was a fair man. She wouldn't want to have to cross him. In fact, she wouldn't want it so much she was rethinking this attraction. Maybe it wasn't such a good idea to have given him her home phone number after all. But what was done was done. Besides, the man wasn't an ogre, just a strong personality. And anyway, who said he would actually call her? She shook her head, and just then Dedrah stepped into the room.

She took one look around and said, "What's wrong?"

"Nothing!" Layne exclaimed brightly. "Nothing at all!" Rod folded his arms, and Sammy glanced up guiltily, giving the lie to her too bright denial. Layne forced herself to relax and, walking swiftly forward, put an arm around Dedrah's shoulders. "I think you're going to be very pleased with the gown. We'll have to schedule several fittings, and I'll want to get your measurements before I start. Can we do that now? It won't take a moment."

"Sure," Dedrah said, eyeing Sammy. "Mind waiting?"

He gave a patient, loving smile. "Nope. Gives me more time to play with our girl." He chucked baby Heather under the chin and laughed at her gurgles. That seemed to ease Dedrah's concerns. She allowed Layne to turn her and guide her back into the fitting room.

Layne made short work of the measurements, performing each one by sheer rote. She'd done it so many times, she could almost do it without thinking. Even double-checking her figures required only mechanical thought. When she and Dedrah returned to the consultation room, both Rod and Sammy were on the floor with the baby. The tension was completely dispelled, and the scene couldn't have looked more cozy. The attraction she felt for Rod Corley burgeoned abruptly, becoming an almost painful yearning that seemed centered heavily in her chest. When he got up, grinning boyishly, and came toward her, she felt herself swaying and put out a hand to steady herself. He folded it in his own much larger one as naturally as if it was something he'd done countless times, and that contact oddly strengthened her. She straightened and composed her features.

"We made real progress today," she said, her voice sounding only slightly strangled.

He nodded. "I'll talk to you soon."

She forced her mouth into a benign smile. "Soon."

He released her and ushered his crew out of the place. What would he have thought, she wondered, if he could have seen her once he was gone, gasping for breath and pressing her hand over her left breast? He would have thought that she was behaving like a schoolgirl with her first crush. And he would have been right. That was the upshot of it. He would have been right. But she was not a schoolgirl, and this was not a crush—and *that* was what frightened her.

Chapter Four

Layne listened to the ringing of the phone without pause. The shop was closed, the answering machine was on and she had to have this gown ready for fitting tomorrow. She supposed she should have let Agnes, her alterations seamstress, stay over and finish the sewing. Agnes could use the overtime and she, Layne, could use some rest, but more than she wanted relaxation, she wanted her mind occupied. She didn't want to think about Rod Corley. She didn't want to wonder what he was doing or if he would call or whether he liked her as much as she thought she liked him; so she kept right on sewing while the phone rang and rang and rang.

Finally her own voice came to her above the sound of the sewing machine, thanking the caller for having reached Harington's Bridal and Formal, stating that their regular hours were 9:00 a.m. to 6:00 p.m., Monday through Saturday, with private consultations available by appointment, and finally advising that name and number be left after the sound of the beep. Several seconds of silence followed. Then came the irritating, mechanical *eeeep* and the one voice that could break her concentration.

"Hi, um, Layne, this is Rod . . . Corley, and, uh, I was wondering . . ." She was up and moving across the room toward the wall phone, willing him not to hang up before she could let him know she was there. "I mean, I need to talk to you about . . . the invitations . . . and, well, I tried calling you at home, but—"

She lifted the receiver and spoke into it. "I'm here, Rod." Her voice played into the room through the answering machine's speaker.

"Oh. Hi."

"Hold on a minute, can you?"

"Sure."

She put down the receiver and raced down the hall and across the consultation room to her desk. Quickly she shut off the answering machine then ran back down the hall and snatched up the receiver once more.

"Back." Her voice was breathless, and she knew it wasn't entirely due to the little jaunt she'd just taken.

"Working late?"

"Afraid so, but I have a few moments."

"Great. But, um, I don't want to take you away from anything important."

"No, it's all right, really. You said something about invitations?"

"Right. Ah, the thing is, I wanted to get this nailed down, you know, and I'm, ah, just no closer to doing that now than I was the other day." He paused for a deep breath. "So, I was hoping we could . . . get together and work on it . . . the two of us."

The two of us. Layne smiled and cupped the telephone with both hands. She cleared her throat. "Sure. Of course. When did you want to . . . get together?"

"Well, as soon as possible."

Her eyes went to the sewing machine and the fabric resting beneath its pressure foot. She had to have that dress ready for fitting by morning. Nevertheless, she heard herself saying, "Why not come over right now? I'll be here a while yet." *Like all night,* she added silently, but the enthusiasm in his voice banished any regret.

"Right now? That's wonderful! You sure it won't be a problem?"

"Not at all."

"I was hoping you'd say that."

"I'll unlock the back door. Just come on into the workroom, all right?"

"Fine. Give me about half an hour."

"Half an hour. Bye."

"Bye."

Layne hung up and glanced around the room, then down at herself. She'd had a light dinner at home, changed into jeans, canvas sneakers and a big, soft sweater, then came straight back here. Using a comb and lipstick from her purse she made some quick repairs on her appearance. Next she concentrated on the workroom, running the carpet sweeper and brushing the cutting and sewing tables free of ravelings and fabric scraps, putting away unused tools, then making a fresh pot of coffee. That done, she made herself sit down and sew. She made only one seam before she heard a light tap, then the opening of the heavy metal door at the back of the building.

"Layne?"

She got up and went to push open one of the three doors that led into the workroom. "Here."

The short hallway was dark, but light slanted through the opened door of the workroom. He stepped into it almost shyly, head bare, a piece of paper in one hand. "Good of you to see me like this," he said quietly.

She smiled. "Glad to help. Come on in." She turned from the doorway, and he moved through it with swift strides. "Want some coffee?"

"If it's no trouble."

"No trouble. I made some fresh for myself a little earlier." She went to the small cabinet in the corner and filled two clean cups. "How do you like it?"

"Black."

She handed over one cup and kept the other for herself. For several seconds they eyed one another over the rims of their cups while they sipped the dark coffee. Then Layne walked to the drawing table and leaned against it, motioning him with a jerk of her head. "Let's see what you've got."

He walked over and spread out the paper with one hand, standing close enough that when he lifted his cup to his mouth once more, his elbow brushed her arm. She leaned forward and peered down at the paper, ignoring the delicious shiver caused by the light contact. He had written three versions of the invitation, one that placed him and Dedrah's parents in the positions of hosts, one that transferred that role to Dedrah and Sam, and one that simply stated the receiver was invited to the wedding of Dedrah and Sam.

"I like this idea best," she said, referring to the last option, "but the wording needs some formality. Let's see . . ." She picked up a hard-leaded pencil from a storage tray and considered for some time before putting it to paper. When she had finished, she read aloud what she had written. "The honor of your presence is happily requested at the wedding ceremony of Dedrah Beverly March and Samuel Calvin Corley on whatever date we decide, whatever time we decide, at whatever place we decide, Duncan, Oklahoma. How does that sound?"

She looked up over her shoulder and met the warmth of approval in his eyes and smile. He set his cup down against the lip of the slightly tilted table and hooked his thumbs in the pockets of his jeans. "That's perfect," he said softly, "just perfect."

Smiling, she left her cup on the table, too, and straightened, turning in the same movement to face him, not a handbreadth between them. "I'm glad you're pleased," she said, "but we'd best fill in those blanks soon so we can get our order in."

"Right. Speaking of orders, you never called about the deposit on that material order."

"Oh, well, I—I didn't really need a deposit." She couldn't say that she'd been afraid she would make a fool of herself if she called him up on the phone, that she'd wanted him to call her if only to prove that he was as anxious to speak to her as she had been to speak to him. "I mean, I can trust you, surely."

"Absolutely," he said, his voice deadly serious. "I would never do anything to hurt you, Layne, not when you've been so kind and helpful and . . ." He bowed his head and lifted a hand to brush his temple on the way to settling it at the back of his neck. Then suddenly he pinned her with a direct, rather pleading look. "You are so unbelievably beautiful!"

That put her heart in her throat and color in her cheeks. She struggled for breath. "You . . . you think so?"

His own breath rushed out, and his mouth crooked up in a smile. "I just said so, didn't I?"

"Yes, you did." She wanted to touch her hair but self-consciously kept her hands at her sides. "Th-thank you. Thank you very much." She dropped her gaze.

"Welcome," he muttered. An awkward silence followed, then, "Whew! I haven't tried to do this in a long time, and I wasn't any good at it then, either!"

She glanced up, then quickly away. "Do what?"

He cleared his throat, shifted his weight, then took a deep breath. "Ask a woman out on a date."

Her mouth dropped open, and her gaze hitched up to fasten on his face. "D-date?"

He lifted his brows hopefully. "I thought maybe a movie..."

A movie date. Good grief, when had she last seen a movie with a man by her side? One thing was certain, she'd been well over sixteen, which was what she felt at the moment. She gulped down a spurt of laughter, delight surging through her, and managed to say, "Th-that would be...wonderful!"

His shoulders sagged with relief, and suddenly they were both laughing. "I'm getting too old for this kind of thing," he said.

"I know what you mean. I was just trying to think when I last went to a movie with a date."

"Oh, I don't even want to go back that far."

"Neither do I."

They laughed again, then sobered. "So, um, what would you like to see?"

She shrugged. "I don't even know what's showing."

"Don't get out much, huh?"

She glanced around her. "Not as much as I should, probably."

He nodded and stepped forward, his hand drifting up to her shoulder. "We're about to change that," he said softly.

She let her gaze dip as low as his mouth, and his hand moved to cup the back of her head. She closed her eyes, and his mouth settled over hers. His lips were soft at first, incredibly so. Then his hand flexed at the back of her head, and his arm slid around her shoulders, his mouth growing firmer as he slanted it across hers. She did not remember reaching around him or locking her fists in the fabric of his shirt. Only after the kiss had slowly melted did she realize that she was hanging on for dear life. He hugged her close, his chin next to her ear, and she released his shirt to flatten her palms against the smooth muscles of his back. He was hard as rock and solid as an oak, and in those few moments she savored the safety and shelter of him before he loosened his hold and carefully stepped back.

"I've wanted to do that since the first moment I laid eyes on you," he said softly. "Thanks."

She merely smiled and nodded, not knowing what to say.

"Well, I'd better get out of here and let you go back to work." He backed away a few steps. "Lock the door again, will you?"

Her smile widened. "Do you try to take care of everyone you know?"

He shook his head. "Just the people I like the most."

"Ah. Then I will definitely lock the door."

"Good." He turned away, then around. "Our date! Will Friday be all right?"

"Friday's fine."

"About eight?"

It hit her suddenly. "You'll need my address."

"Oh, right!"

She turned back to the drawing table, tore a corner off the piece of paper he'd brought with him, scribbled her address on it and carried it to him. He glanced at it and slid it into his shirt pocket.

"Eight on Friday," she reiterated.

He nodded and went out the door, his strides carrying him quickly beyond the slant of the light. She heard the knob turn on the metal outer door, then his voice from the dark at the end of the hall. "Good night, good-looking." She smiled and lifted a hand in farewell, holding it until she heard the door open and close again, then laying it over her heart.

Rod found the small, low, ranch-style house in a neatly manicured neighborhood on the north side of town, just east of the 81 Bypass. It was the kind of place where couples settled to raise families then stayed on to enjoy their retirement. The properties were well cared for but unpretentious, solidly middle-class and unashamed of it. Even in the dark with the crispness of fall in the air, the neighborhood radiated the cozy serenity and orderliness of a safe haven. It was somehow exactly the sort of place where he had pictured Layne Harington residing.

The house itself was solidly built of beige brick with a narrow, ground-level porch running the full length of the front. Pots of ivy hung at regular intervals beneath the eaves of the roof, and a low, thick hedge of shrubs bordered the foundation. Narrow flower beds edged the walkway that ran from the porch to the street. On one side of the yard, a large weeping willow spread its drooping branches, swaying gracefully in the gentle wind. Opposite it, a large black cauldron frothed with greenery and the closed buds of autumn flowers, while two large lilac bushes played sentries at the outside corners of the porch. Layne obviously lavished attention on her home, and it seemed that everything to which she put her hand thrived.

He had never known a woman quite like her. She was accomplished, creative, even artistic; yet she possessed no flightiness, no arrogance, no aberrant moodiness. She was instead an intelligent, steady, classy, caring, deliciously attractive woman, and he hadn't wanted so much for a female to like him since he'd turned twenty—and that had been as many years ago. In truth, he had given up on dating by the time he'd reached thirty-five. The women he'd met just had not inspired in him any real devotion, but something told him that Layne might be different. It frightened him a little, having his hopes raised, and the funny thing was that he didn't even know for what he was hoping.

He knew he was something of a loner. He had been content to concentrate on reviving the family ranch even before his late brother's son had come into his life. Still, he had enjoyed having Sammy with him. They were a family, just the two of them, and now there was Dedrah and Heather. And yet, he suddenly felt more alone than ever before. He watched Sammy with Heather sometimes, saw how protective and adoring he was, ever alert for what was best and right for his little girl, and he saw himself in Sammy's place and Sam in Heather's, and he knew he couldn't love Sammy more if he were his own son. But it was not enough. It was what Sammy had with Dedrah that Rod envied—the quiet sense of belonging in the same place at the same time with someone else, the acceptance of responsibility that had to be granted rather than inherited, the fulfilling of need by choice and not compulsion. It was very odd, for he was not at all the romantic sort, and empty lust had lost its fascination long, long ago, but the moment he had met Layne Harington, everything male in him had intensified, and he had begun to think of *not* being alone.

It was a lot to think about, a lot to struggle with, and he was still doing both as he walked up the arrow-straight, hedged concrete path to her front door. His heart was pounding, his palms sweaty, his mouth dry, his ears ringing; he had never been so eager for anything as he was for this evening. It made no sense, and he was used to his life making sense. He had worked hard for that very thing, harder than anyone knew, but here he was, knocking on her door. He had barely lifted his knuckles from the green painted door when it opened, and she stood there smiling at him, dressed in a peacock blue turtleneck sweater and a straight plaid skirt, white and burgundy and yellow-gold on a blue background. He wondered where she had found stockings and shoes of that exact same shade of peacock blue, and then he remembered the remarkable number of resources that lay at her fingertips in the bridal and formal shop where he had first seen her. Her stockings would always match. Attention to detail was part of her charm.

"Come in," she said simply.

He stepped over the threshold and looked around the living room while she closed the door. The carpet was teal and thick underfoot. The sofa, armchairs and ottoman were covered in a gold fabric that was tweedy in texture, and there were pillows of various muted colors in shiny cotton fabric scattered everywhere. The drapes were flowered in large splashes of subtle shades on a teal background and trimmed with gold braid. It was a clean, orderly, comfortable room with blond woods and, incredibly, soft violet-gray walls. It was the kind of place where one could entertain country-club cronies or put bare feet up and read the newspaper. He liked it immensely and told her so. "Your home's almost as lovely as you."

She laughed in a burst of sound. "You say the most outrageous things."

"Do I?"

"I'm afraid so."

"Sorry."

"Goodness, don't apologize. I love it."

"Oh. Well, then I'm not sorry."

She laughed again, a husky chuckle that made him smile. "Sit down, and we'll look at the movie listings. Would you like something to drink? I've mulled some cider."

"Really? I've never had it before, but I suppose that's what smells so wonderful."

"Yes, apples and cinnamon and butter, with a touch of clove."

"Sounds great. I'll have some."

She motioned him down onto the sofa on her way out of the room. Moments later she returned with two smoked glass cups three-quarters full of a steaming amber liquid. He accepted one and leaned forward, elbows on knees, to study the newspaper opened to the right page and folded on the sturdy coffee table. The aroma wafting up to him reminded him of Christmas and Thanksgiving and a Yule log on a blazing fire. He sipped and found the cider scalding, sticky sweet and thoroughly delicious.

"This is good," he said. "You'll have to tell me how you make this."

She shrugged. "Cider, spiced apple rings, cinnamon sticks and cloves set to simmer over a low flame. Pour it in a cup, and add a dollop of butter. Holidays, my dad adds a few drops of brandy.''

He grinned around the rim of his cup. ''Holidays are exactly what it makes me think of.''

She nodded her understanding. ''Have you found a movie you'd like to see?''

He turned his attention back to the paper and read off the listings. ''I'll go for anything but silly movies.''

She wrinkled her nose. ''They don't appeal to me, either, but neither do the cops and robbers.''

''Scratch the cops,'' he said. ''Of the remaining three, the first one starts in exactly one hour.''

''Sounds good to me.''

That settled, they leaned back to sip cider. He asked how long she'd lived here. She told him, then explained how her father had helped her shop for the house, how excited she had been to find it, what changes she'd made. They refilled their cups and talked about his house, which according to him was far less comfortable than hers. Then he glanced at his watch and found the first movie was about to start.

''Maybe if we hurry,'' he said, but she shook her head unconcernedly.

''We can go to the second one. That gives us an extra half hour.''

He found her calmness steadying. ''Excellent idea.''

She went to get a jacket and her handbag. He jumped up and helped her into the wine-red coat, then escorted her out the door and down the walk to his truck. He let her in on the passenger side, then walked around and slid under the wheel. He turned the truck around in her drive and headed it back the way he'd come. Five minutes later, he was parking in front of the theater.

"We still have a few minutes," he said. "Want to wait here or go on in?"

"Here's fine."

He was glad she didn't want to go in yet. He liked having her all to himself, liked talking to her, listening to her. To make that happen, he asked about her family. She had already mentioned her father twice, and now she talked effortlessly about her mother, two brothers and two sisters, aunts, uncles, cousins. He envied her wealth of kin and obvious fondness of them, because on his side it really was just him and Sam. He explained that his only brother, Sammy's father, had died in a drunk driving accident before Sammy was born. For three years, Sammy had lived with his grandparents and mother. Then his mother had drowned and his grandmother had suffered a stroke, and Sammy had come to him. Both his grandparents were now deceased as well. Layne said it sounded terribly lonely, but he told her it was nothing of the kind. It was, instead, simple and cementing. He and Sammy would always be close. She could understand that. She understood it so well that the next time he thought to check the time, the second movie was well under way!

Apologizing profusely, he went up to the ticket window to check out the remaining options, but the next showing of anything they both wanted to see was at midnight. He felt like an idiot, but Layne laughed at him, saying, "If we hadn't been enjoying ourselves so much already, we wouldn't have lost track of time. I suggest a cup of coffee to hold us over to the midnight showing."

It was an enjoyable proposal. He drove them down the 81 Bypass to a local coffee shop, and there they resumed their conversation. The topic this time was favorite movies of the past, and from there they moved to books.

Along about eleven, his stomach started to rumble, and after much chuckling and discussion they decided to have dessert, only Rod decided to have his with a club sandwich, which they wound up sharing. By the time they'd finished eating, Rod glanced at his wrist and was stunned to find that midnight had come and gone. He removed his watch and slid it across the table silently, a relatively simple procedure as the gold band released with the lift of a latch, unlike the black leather band with buckle that he wore every day.

Layne put down her water glass and studied the face of the watch four full seconds, then her eyes wandered up, and her teeth caught the corner of her full lower lip. Abruptly her gaze switched to his face, and those green eyes sparkled with such mirth that he found himself sputtering laughter. Her own laughter, barely held in check until that moment, joined his. Heads turned. Curious glances moved over them. As one, they stifled their outburst, subsiding into snickers and squeaks.

Rod felt curiously elated, though at any other time and with anyone else he would have been annoyed. He was beginning to understand how deeply and in how many ways this woman could affect him. The hilarity mastered, he said quietly, "Obviously we weren't meant to see a movie tonight. I hope you don't mind."

She shook her head, her smile still wide. "I've had a lovely time, but would you think I'm a glutton if we ordered another sandwich? I was too nervous earlier to eat my dinner."

It was a charming confession, and he did not want the evening to end just yet. Her hand lay atop his watch, and he covered it with his own, squeezing gently. She turned her palm up and clasped his fingers. For a long moment, he studied her gold-green eyes, unable to look away, desperately wondering what she was thinking, what she expected, what she hoped for with him. Suddenly he knew what he wanted from Layne Harington. He wanted her caring, her passion, her serenity, her love. But love wasn't as simple as a club sandwich. Love was as complicated as the people involved, and he was terribly complicated, too complicated for most women. How much more so for a simple, straightforward, orderly woman like Layne? Dismay filled him—dark, lonely, heavy. He took his hand from hers and lifted it to signal the waitress.

The sandwich was ordered, delivered and eaten, though his share tasted like cardboard in his mouth. He knew his sudden shift in mood was stifling the conversation, ruining the enjoyment, confusing his companion, but having realized the risk he was taking, he was uncertain if he wanted to pursue this relationship. If he let himself love her, would she respond in kind, only to turn away later? His background was ugly and convoluted. Because of it he fought battles daily that other people did not even consider.

The situation with Sam and Dedrah was but one example of the sort of thing that typified his life. Could Layne deal with that? Would he really want his wife to have to deal with it? Life was hard when you had to hold up your head and stare down the rest of the world every day, and this mess with Sammy had proven to him that he couldn't protect those he loved from the particular affliction that haunted the Corley family. He had wanted so much to spare Sammy the shame he himself had known as a young man! And if he couldn't spare Sammy, he couldn't spare anyone else.

When the waitress came with a fresh pot of coffee, he covered his cup with his hand. Layne smiled and shook her head at the waitress. She carried the pot away, and a few minutes later returned with their check. He excused himself and slipped out of the booth to pay the cashier. When he returned, he slid a few bucks under the rim of his plate for the waitress, a generous tip for tying up her table so long. Then he slid a hand under Layne's elbow, helping her maneuver free of the booth and stand. When he lightly pressed his hand against the small of her back, she bowed her head and walked smoothly out of the building.

She was silent as he drove her home, merely nodding or smiling wanly in response to his careful attempts at making conversation. He knew he had hurt her with his sudden withdrawal, but how much more would he hurt her if he did not withdraw? As so often in the past, he felt cheated by his heritage, and once again bitter self-pity overwhelmed him. He discovered that he could not shake it off so easily as usual, and falling silent, he abandoned his efforts to comfort her, directing his energy instead toward tempering his own feelings of guilt, frustration and loss. He had almost achieved that liberating numbness in which he'd lived so much of his life when they arrived at her place. He turned the truck into the drive this time, shut off the engine and was reaching for the door handle when she stopped him with a hand on his forearm. Automatically he fixed a questioning gaze on her, only to find it returned with double intensity.

"Did I do something wrong?" she asked, a catch in her small voice.

Regret assailed him. "No! Good heavens, no." He leaned toward her, one elbow on the back of the seat, the other balanced against the steering wheel. He owed her an explanation, if only he could find the words for it.

"You're wonderful," he told her. "You're not the problem at all." But she shook her head, eyelids shuttering.

"You don't have to say that. I shouldn't have asked. Nothing like putting your date in the hot seat to wrap up a perfect evening . . . almost perfect."

Just the sound of her voice was heartrendingly poignant, the bald hope laced with deep disappointment. Instinctively he reached out a hand in comfort, but the moment his fingertips touched her cheek, he knew it was a mistake. Energy coursed up his arm, a strange magnetism that compelled him to cup his palm about her jaw. Her eyelids lifted slowly, and her face tilted upward, her gaze settling upon his mouth. It was as clear a signal as a man could expect, and he simply didn't have it in him to ignore it. He slid his hand down and around her neck and across her shoulder, pulling her to him.

She came into his arms without the slightest hesitation, her head falling back as her mouth rose to meet his. Sweet, soft, so precious, she offered up her heart and her hope and the promise of all-consuming passion. For a long, heady moment he could only answer her in kind, his mouth moving over hers as his arms folded her tightly against him. Her arms crept up around his neck, and her body melted into the curve of his, her gentle warmth suffusing him. It was sweet, so very sweet. And then her mouth parted, and her tongue stroked timidly against his teeth, awakening needs he had not truly known existed in him. Suddenly nothing mattered but having those needs met, having the hurt soothed, the passion matched, the emptiness filled.

He thrust his legs out and leaned back, pulling her atop him, their bodies wedged between the seat and the steering wheel. Her hands invaded his hair and dipped low along his spine. Groaning, he slid his own hands down to her hips, lifted and positioned her, and pressed her hard against him, making known his desire with brutal honesty. At once, he realized he had gone too far. She stiffened, and her hands retreated. Finally she broke apart the kiss, gasping and turning her face into the crook of his neck. He folded his arms about her waist, apologizing and comforting. After a moment, she angled her body sideways and lifted her head to gaze down at his regretful face. To his amazement, her mouth quirked in a smile, her fingertips brushing his temple.

"I haven't ever felt this way before," she said softly. "I like it, but I think I should tell you, I won't sleep with you unless we get married."

Just like that, she laid out the perimeter of this thing between them and labeled it boldly. She liked him and was not indifferent sexually. She might even come to love him and, if convinced that he returned her feelings, would marry him. And then, but only then, would she gift him with her body and her self. It was as if she had set his feet firmly beneath him once more and pointed him in the safest direction. They would go slowly, carefully, until they arrived at the point of certainty, where they would either join or part by mutual consent. One need not hurt the other unbearably. Feelings need not be risked unrequited. It was so wonderfully sensible, so safely sane.

He rose to a sitting position, carrying her with him, and kissed the top of her head and the curve of her cheekbone before tasting her mouth once more. He played the kiss out and stroked her sleek, chestnut hair, smiling down into trusting green eyes.

"Let's make another go at that movie," he said. "Tomorrow night?"

She beamed at him, her hand finding and curling into his. "Tomorrow night," she said, and he smiled the smile of the grateful, laughter once more just below the surface. It did not have to end in disaster, and in the meantime, he need not be so very alone. If it was less than he wanted, well, there was hope of more, and he knew it was all he could ask for. Hope. Hope of love.

Chapter Five

They saw the movie. Rod had made certain that they wouldn't miss it. When he picked her up, he didn't come in for conversation or cider or anything else, insisting instead that they should go on to the theater and buy their tickets. They waited in the lobby for the feature to start, munching popcorn and sipping soft drinks. Afterward, he took her straight home and stood protectively on her front porch while she unlocked the door and flipped on the lights. Then he gave her a gentlemanly kiss, declined "with regret" an invitation for coffee, and left her.

Layne feared that she had failed some test, that he would not call again, and for several days he did not. On the following Wednesday, however, he strode into the shop with Dedrah in tow, and his smile of greeting was warm and personal, his eyes full of promise. When she offered him her hand, he clasped it in both of his own, then tucked it into the fold of his elbow as they reclaimed the consultation room. The faint gloom that had descended the previous Saturday night evaporated, allowing Layne to turn her mind to business without distraction.

"I have a specific date," she said, "providing we can agree on sites. The First Church of Duncan has an open date on Saturday the fifteenth. It's a lovely building, and I know both the pastor, Bolton Charles, and his wife, Carol. I'm sure you'll like them. Bolton's my favorite among the clergy here because of his tact and thoughtfulness, and Carol is kind and unassuming. Now, the church requires a cleaning deposit of a hundred dollars for nonmembers. They will take the cost of the cleanup out of that and refund the rest, or you can arrange the cleanup yourselves and have the whole deposit refunded. I suggest you let them do it because it will be one less detail we have to deal with. Well, what do you say?"

Rod looked at Dedrah, who lifted her shoulders unconcernedly. "Sounds okay to me."

Layne could only wonder at such lack of enthusiasm. Most brides wanted every detail perfect, but Dedrah remained singularly uninvolved. Didn't Rod wonder about that, too? Maybe he didn't realize her reaction was odd. He did not, after all, have Layne's vast experience with this kind of thing. Should she say something to him? Was it possible that after all her hard work, Dedrah would change her mind? Surely not. She shook her head, then realizing how it must look to the others, quickly said, "It's your wedding, Dedrah. I want you to be pleased. Maybe you'd like to see pictures of the church?" Without waiting for a reply, she opened one of the folders on the table in front of her and extracted three snapshots, which she placed in front of Dedrah.

The girl dutifully looked them over, nodded and smiled. "It's very pretty. I like it."

Tepid as that pronouncement was, it relieved Layne greatly. At least Dedrah didn't hate the place. She looked to Rod for reinforcement and was not disappointed. He studied the photos solemnly, then handed them back to her. "It's perfect," he said. "You chose well. Thank you."

"It's settled, then?"

"Settled," Rod confirmed.

Layne looked at Dedrah, and the girl nodded. Layne felt as if she'd reached the summit of a mountain climb, but she was far from finished. "Now the reception," she began. "There are banquet facilities on the church grounds, but one of the better hotels in town is also available, and as they offer a catering service, it would simplify matters greatly—"

"I think you're right," Rod broke in. "Let's use them."

"I ought to warn you, though," she insisted, "they're expensive."

He waved a hand negligently. "I told you before, money's the least of my concerns."

"You wouldn't say that if you had to do without it," Dedrah whispered timidly.

Rod opened his mouth in shock, then chuckled and ruffled her hair with his big hand as if she were a tot. "Sugar, you have no way of knowing what I've done without in my lifetime, and I hope you never do. Besides, I'd give everything I have to get you and Sam off to a good start." Dedrah looked appalled, and he quickly added, "but it won't come to that, believe me. I've been socking money away for years. A good chunk of it was meant for Sammy's college education, but when he chose the military instead, I decided to make it a wedding present. Didn't figure to spend it quite this way, but I'm sure there'll be some left over to help you set up housekeeping.''

Dedrah looked away, her face bleak, but then she carefully arranged a smile on her lips and turned it up to him. ''Thank you,'' she said, her voice wavering a little. ''You're very generous, and Sam and I know you have our best at heart.''

Rod patted her shoulder gently, then turned his attention to Layne. ''What next, mastermind?''

She smiled at him. ''Time. I suggest no earlier than 6:30 p.m. for a formal ceremony, no later than eight.''

Dedrah looked dismayed. ''I was kind of thinking daytime.''

''If that's what you want, that's what we'll do,'' Layne said, not in the least disturbed. Quite the contrary, she was delighted to find that Dedrah had some preference in this. ''We can do a morning wedding followed by a luncheon, or an afternoon wedding followed by dinner. It's up to you.''

Rod casually laid his hands on the tabletop and looked at Dedrah. ''I thought I heard Sammy say something the other evening about a candlelight ceremony,'' he said lightly.

Dedrah frowned, her winged brows drawing together in the center. ''You're right. He did say a candlelight service would be nice.'' She looked at Layne, her gaze apologetic and oddly removed. ''I guess we'd better do it after dark. About seven maybe?''

Layne peered at her closely. ''Are you sure?'' The girl nodded, and her face set with resolve. Layne mentally shrugged. ''All right. Now we can order the invitations and go on to choosing music, food and flowers.''

''Music,'' Dedrah muttered. ''Oh, my. I hadn't thought of that.''

"Well, start thinking about it," Layne said. "You'll need a minimum of three pieces for the ceremony. I have a list of suggestions for a formal service and a tape you can listen to. My personal favorites are 'Spring' from Vivaldi's *The Four Seasons* and Walton's 'Coronation March,' and of course we can always do the traditional 'Bridal Chorus,' but some people think it's kind of cheesy now. Do you have anyone in mind as a soloist? If not, I know a marvelous soprano we can probably get for a reasonable fee. Oh, and her husband's an excellent organist, too. They have a lovely pipe organ at the First Church, small but perfectly pitched. We might want to contact a trumpeter, too, and maybe a flautist."

"Flautist?" Dedrah echoed uncertainly.

"A flute player," Rod clarified, and Dedrah rolled her eyes.

"Holy smoke!"

Rod laughed indulgently. "Just leave it to the pro," he advised. "Layne won't steer us wrong."

His eyes, warm and confident, traveled to Layne's face, and she felt herself blush. "We'll come back to the flau...flutist later. Now about the reception, will you want dancing?" Receiving an affirmative reply from Dedrah herself, Layne talked nonstop for twenty minutes, describing local bands and musicians and the types of music performed by each. Dedrah was surprisingly adamant about country music being played at the reception, and Rod agreed that it was the most popular option, but Layne merely smiled at Dedrah's assertion that a jukebox would be just fine. "I know a very good five-piece band," she said, "and they owe me a favor. Let's start there and see what we come up with." She closed the notebook in which she'd been making notes and gave Dedrah a cassette that was on the table. "I think that's about it for now. Listen to the tape and let me know what you think next time. Shall we say Monday, around four?''

"Fine," Rod replied. He laid a hand on Dedrah's shoulder. "Excuse us a minute, hon. I have something personal to discuss with Layne."

She gave him a measuring look, then smiled, nodded and got up to walk away. Layne could feel her heartbeat in the hollow of her throat. "Personal?" she asked, inwardly wincing at the thin, strident sound of her own voice. "What personal something did you want to discuss?"

"Dinner," he said quietly. "Friday at seven-thirty?"

She didn't realize until that moment that she had unconsciously feared what he might have to say. Had she really expected him to break it off? Deep down, no, and yet some part of her had obviously wondered if he might have resented her announcement about sex waiting for marriage. Apparently not, and she couldn't have been more pleased, especially as she remembered how he'd kissed her that first night. There had been a world of wanting in that kiss, enough to fill her dreams ever since. Remembering those dreams, she blushed again. Though she bowed her head, Rod's sharp eyes caught the rising color, and his hand came out to cover hers.

"What's this? Embarrassed about a simple dinner invitation?"

"Of c-course not," she managed. "It's just..." Unable to come up with a totally false explanation, she settled for near truth. "I—I was beginning to wonder if you wanted to see me again."

He had the grace not to laugh, but she saw the impulse there in his eyes when she looked up at him. He shook his head, his mouth quirking. "You couldn't be more wrong," he said evenly. "In fact, I was going to suggest Friday that we drive over to the Wichita Mountains on Saturday afternoon. It's not too cold yet for a picnic."

She beamed and knew her gaze was filled with relieved delight. "I'd like that very much—provided I can pack the picnic."

He laughed then. "I was hoping you'd say that." His expression changed, and he squeezed her hand. "But you haven't accepted my invitation to dinner on Friday. I hope that doesn't mean—"

"I'd love to have dinner with you on Friday," she interrupted.

"Great! Seven-thirty?"

"Seven-thirty."

He got up and, before she could also rise, dropped a kiss on the top of her head. "Nothing fancy," he said, walking backward. He named a good restaurant downtown. She nodded her agreement, her heart in her throat, and he winked before leaving her.

She sat where she was, aware that the whole shop now knew she was seeing Rod Corley, and not caring a whit. Indeed, she felt rather smug about it, and why shouldn't she? He was hugely attractive, generous to a fault, engaging, intelligent, overtly masculine. He was very nearly perfect. Undoubtedly he could have his pick of women, and yet he'd chosen her to receive his attention. She hugged that knowledge to herself and held it there all during the weeks to follow.

It was late, and Layne was tired, but work had piled up while she had been out and about with Rod Corley. Rod. She couldn't think of him without smiling. She wondered if it was too soon to introduce him to her family.

They knew about him, of course. How could they not, with him taking up so much of her time these past five weeks? Still, she had never really discussed him with them, and were she to do so, she didn't know what she would say. She and Rod had seen a good deal of each other, and yet it was almost as it had been in the beginning with them. They went out, and they enjoyed one another's company, but nothing had happened between them that was more intimate than what had happened in front of her house that very first night. Yet, when he did touch her in small, casual ways—a handclasp, the brush of fingertips on her cheek or brow, the draping of an arm about her shoulders—the moment invariably seemed charged with promise and possibility. Perhaps he was waiting for her to make the next move, and if that was the case, then introducing him to her family might be just the thing. But if so, then why did it seem so... presumptuous?

She sighed. This was not getting work done, and work had to be the priority for the moment. Perhaps she should take on another seamstress, but seamstresses of the necessary caliber were few and far between. Not even Agnes could do everything that needed doing, which meant she had best buckle down and take care of all these matters Agnes could not. With Herculean effort, she made herself concentrate on the pattern she was sewing for cutout, but not thirty seconds later a loud, hollow banging sounded at the back door. Momentarily alarmed, she wondered if she ought to call someone, but then Rod's muffled voice reached her.

"Layne? It's me, honey. Open up."

A thrill swept through her. If he could be moved to impulsive action at this point, perhaps things were further along than she had imagined. She abandoned the

sewing and got to her feet, swiftly crossing to the door
that led into the back hallway. She switched on the light
there and literally ran to throw the bolt and open the
outside door. He stepped up and swept past her without
a word, striding heavily for the workroom.

She bit her lip. What could be wrong? She didn't have
to ask. He threw up his arms the instant she stepped into
the room and spat it out.

"I will never understand that kid! I raised him, and
he's like a stranger to me!"

Sammy. She automatically relaxed, sensing that her
steadiness was what he needed now. "I've heard my parents say that very thing," she offered quietly.

He shot her a skeptical glance. "Really?"

She nodded, glad beyond words that he'd come to her
like this. She walked to the beverage cabinet and poured
him a cup of coffee. "I think there comes a time in every
parent/child relationship when the child is a stranger to
the parent. It has something to do with the metamor-
phosis to maturity. Once it's complete, everything's familiar again. At least, that's what my parents say."

He ran his hand through his hair before taking the cup.
"I hope they're right about that," he rumbled, "but I
wouldn't bank on it just now."

She placed her hand on his forearm and tugged him
toward a chair. "Tell me about it."

He dropped down heavily and seemed to ponder where
to begin. She waited silently, and he finally found his
place. "I want what's best for them," he told her unnec-
essarily, "and I've thought about this a great deal. I want
him to adopt Heather rather than simply acknowledge
her, but you'd think I was asking him to abandon her by
the roadside!"

Layne was momentarily stunned, then merely confused. Adopt his own child? It didn't make sense. She shook her head. "I'm afraid I don't understand."

He grimaced and shot up to his feet, sloshing coffee over his hand. She reached out for the cup, and he let go of it absently. "It would look better for everyone," he said, then he immediately backpedaled. "All right, it would look better for Sammy. I can admit I think of him first, and why shouldn't I? He's come first with me since he was four years old. Besides the damage is already done as far as Dedrah is concerned. She wasn't married when Heather was born, and nothing will change that."

Layne sat with her mouth open, staring at him. She could hardly believe what he was suggesting or the level of desperation with which he was suggesting it. She cleared her throat, choosing her words carefully. "If Sammy adopts Heather rather than acknowledging her, people will assume he's not her natural father. He'll look the part of hero, marrying Dedrah despite her, ah, indiscretion and accepting her illegitimate child as his own. I assume Dedrah would go along. She obviously loves Sammy without reservation. But Sammy has apparently balked. Now why would he do that? I wonder if he is motivated by a misguided sense of honor? Or just simple decency?"

Rod looked positively stricken. "You're right, of course," he whispered. "Dear God, what was I thinking? No wonder he was so angry with me. It's just... He doesn't know what they'll be saying about him. I should have told him, but somehow I couldn't. There seemed no point in it. How could I know this would happen?"

Misery was written all over him, and Layne knew she didn't understand everything that lay behind his words, but still she felt immense relief that he'd seen the folly in his thinking. Also, she had never wanted anything so much as she wanted to help him now. She got up and carried the coffee cup to the counter, abandoning it there to turn and fold her arms. "Why don't you tell me everything?" she urged quietly. "A burden shared is a burden lightened."

He passed a hand over his eyes wearily, then grasped the chair and turned it around so that he could straddle it and rest his arms along the edge of the back. "There are several things Sammy doesn't know," he began. "For one thing, his mother was married to another man when my brother got her pregnant. Barry didn't love her, but he loved his reputation as a ladies' man, so he bragged about his 'accomplishment.' Her husband left her, and Barry let her move in with us until the baby was born, but he didn't marry her. When she figured out he wasn't going to, she went back home to her parents. Barry continued seeing her, though, and I think she still held out hope. Less than a year later, he was killed in an accident. Sammy's mother committed suicide, but Sam doesn't know that, either."

"Poor Sammy," she whispered.

Rod went on dispassionately. "He stayed with her parents. Then, when he was three, his grandmother had a stroke. I tried to help out as much as I could, and for a while his grandfather managed to care for both of them, but then he died just after Sammy's fourth birthday. My father had died by then, too, but that's another story. I took Sammy home with me and did the best I could by him."

"Of course you did."

He tossed her a cryptic look. "You're the only person ever to say that to me. Back then most people seemed to think it was rather eccentric of me because I was a man

alone and because I had no legal tie to him." He sighed
and rubbed his hand over his face, looking away
quickly—but not before she saw the sheen of tears in his
eyes. When he spoke again, his voice was choked and
thick. "We kept pretty much to ourselves, but that didn't
keep me from hearing what people were saying. When I
enrolled him in first grade, even the principal asked as
smooth as you please why I'd taken on my brother's
bastard." His eyes flashed angrily. "Sam will never know
how hard I fought that label. I threatened. I begged. I
argued. I even took my fists to a few with especially loud
mouths. Eventually, we just outlived the gossip, but
now..." His voice wavered, and he paused to clear his
throat. "Now," he went on wearily, "they'll be talking
about the Corleys again, and this time they'll be saying
Sam's just like his father."

"And you'll be fighting for him again," she added
softly.

He sat very still, his square jaw hardening. "It isn't
fair," he whispered finally. "Barry was a sorry excuse for
a human being, but Sam isn't like that. Sam's—"

"Like you," she said. His smoky blue eyes rose to her
face and held there, such a wealth of yearning in them
that she started forward before she even realized what she
was doing. He stood and stepped over the chair, his arms
opening wide. She walked into them and laid her cheek
against his chest as he wrapped his arms about her, her
head tucked beneath his chin.

"He'll be all right," she said, her voice muffled by the
hollow of his shoulder. "He's strong like you, and the
protection you've already given him will help. So will
your support. The whole town will know you're standing by him. The wedding will prove that."

"I hope so," he said fiercely. "It would just be so much easier for him the other way."

"I don't think so." She tilted her head back so that she could look up into his face. "I meant it when I said he was like you. Now ask yourself, Rod, if you were in Sammy's place, could you deny Heather and play hero to Dedrah's scarlet woman?"

He looked down at her for a long while, then slowly lowered his head and kissed her lips before laying his cheek alongside hers. "No," he said. "I couldn't, and if I'd thought of it that way, I'd have known he couldn't, either."

"But you were thinking like a father," she said softly, mindful that her mouth was close to his ear, "and that's understandable, isn't it?"

He pulled back and smiled at her. "I knew I came to the right person."

She thought her heart would fly right out of her chest. "I'm glad you think so, because I wouldn't want you to go to anyone else."

He caressed her cheek, lightly rubbing his knuckles against her skin, but she wanted more, so much more. Just once she wanted him to kiss her again as he had that first night. Impulsively, she went up on tiptoe and brought her mouth to his, her arms coming around his neck. She pressed herself to him, marveling at her own boldness. Well, why not? How was he going to know how she felt if she didn't show him? They were adults. They'd been seeing each other for some weeks now. And she, for one, was falling in love. It was time he understood that.

If she was a little frantic in her effort to communicate her feelings and desires to him, he seemed not to be in his response. He rested his hands lightly at her waist, and let her take his mouth and press her body to him, but it was not the response she wanted. Where was the fire she had felt that first night? Could he bank it so easily? If so, his feelings for her were not what hers were for him. She'd meant what she'd said. She wouldn't sleep with him unless they married, but blast it, she wanted to! Didn't he understand that? Apparently not, for after a few seconds he set her aside, his hands tugging her arms away from his neck.

"Thank you," he said softly, "but I won't keep you any longer. You need to get back to work, and I need to talk to Sam."

She nodded, covering her devastation with the serene mask that came so easily. *Thank you.* She had done her level best to strike sparks off the man and he coolly thanked her. She folded her arms about her middle and tried to soothe the knot that was twisting there.

"I—I'll see you out."

"And lock the door."

She shook her head cryptically. "I always lock the door."

He smiled sheepishly at that. "Habit," he said, reaching for her hand. She delivered it into his, trying not to react to the waves of excitement that accompanied his touch, and let him lead her out into the hall. At the door, he paused and turned back, taking both her hands this time. "Do you ever get tired of saying good-night?" he asked huskily.

Hope surged, and she turned her face up to study his expression. "Yes. Yes, I do."

He released her, and his hands came up to touch her face, his fingertips patting gently along the curves of her jaws. "Can't be helped, though, can it?"

"I guess not," she answered in a near whisper. A trembling started in the nether reaches of her body, and she felt herself swaying toward him. He frowned, and she forced herself upright, but in that same instant one hand slid around to the back of her head and the other fell to her waist. She caught her breath, knowing what was coming.

Even as his mouth came down over hers, she felt suspended, waiting, and then he jerked her hard against him, his hand sliding down to splay over the full, round curves of her hips. She felt her heart knock hard against the wall of her chest, and her breath rushed out. He captured it and drew it in, then quick as a cat his tongue darted between her parted lips and plumbed the depths of her mouth, sweeping its silken walls and painting its arched roof, stroking with hypnotic insistence her own undulating tongue, then plunging downward as his hand cupped the back of her head and tilted it to suit him.

Her own hands were clamped over the tops of his shoulders, and she had no idea how they'd gotten there, but when he wrapped his arm about her waist and pulled her so tight against him that her back bowed and only her toes remained in contact with the floor, she slid them up and around his neck, flattening her body against him from thigh to breast. His mouth suddenly left hers and found the sensitive flesh along the cord of her neck, just below her ear. Moist heat exploded within her skin and flashed downward, congealing in the pit of her belly. She gasped, and his mouth returned to hers, plundering boldly, greedily, as his hands slid over her body, pulling and pressing as he twisted to bring contact where he wanted it, and everywhere contact was made, it was electric, explosive, searing. She felt him quaking with the power of it, and wondered that it didn't shatter both of them. Then abruptly he was pushing her away, his hands clamped to her upper arms, lungs gasping for air.

"God, I'm sorry! I didn't mean for that to happen! I've been congratulating myself on being so good, and suddenly it gets all out of hand! Believe me, darlin', I won't—"

She put her hand over his mouth, cutting off the flow of apologetic words. "It's all right," she said softly.

He pulled her hand away. "It's not—"

She put it right back again. "Yes, it is! Or don't you remember that I was the one doing the kissing a minute ago?"

He subsided, pushing air out through his nostrils, and she dropped her hand. "That was different," he argued gently, his hands resting warmly at her waist.

"I don't see how," she told him, then she laughed softly. "Well, all right, maybe it was a little different, but that doesn't mean it was bad—or unwelcome, for that matter."

His face split into a grin. "I did notice that."

"All right, then. What's the problem?"

"The problem," he said, sobering, "is that I get carried away when I start touching you."

A thrill of delight shot through her, followed swiftly by a swell of deep satisfaction. She had a hard time keeping the smile off her face. "I don't mind," she said quietly, hitching up a shoulder.

"Don't you?" he replied doubtfully.

She shook her head. "I know you wouldn't do anything I didn't want you to do."

"Not at the moment, maybe," he said gently, "but later it could be very different. Someone has to be sensible, don't you think?"

She bit her lip, knowing he was right, but she didn't want him to be sensible. She wanted him as churned up as she was, though where that might lead she didn't want to contemplate.

Rod lifted a hand to caress her cheek, then dropped it and straightened, reaching toward the doorknob. He turned it, pushed the door open and slipped through. "I'll call you tomorrow."

She managed a smile. "Right."

He paused there a moment longer, his expression distorted by the shadows cast by the strong overhead light. Then he slowly pushed the door closed. Layne leaned against it and shot the bolt, listening to the sounds of his leaving, the quiet fall of footsteps, the muted scraping of hinges, the bump of a closing car door and finally the whine and rumble of an engine coming to life. She put her back to the door and listened until the crunch of tires on pavement faded away into the distance. Only then did she push away and saunter idly down the hall to the workroom.

He wasn't indifferent after all. He was just being careful, prudent, thoughtful. She started to laugh silently. If only he knew how reckless he made her feel at times, and how much she had wanted to see that recklessness reflected in him. She had meant what she'd said about not sleeping with him unless they should happen to marry, but it was so good to know that he wanted her. She had begun to fear that his reserve meant disenchantment. Now she could tell herself otherwise, at least for a while, and hope that eventually his feelings would deepen into something genuine and permanent.

Chapter Six

Layne carefully pinched the fabric, bringing it tight against Dedrah's impossibly small waist. Even before she inserted the pin, Dedrah flinched, then sighed heavily. The tension Layne had been struggling to dispel from the first moments of this fitting thickened perceptively. Layne bit down on the pins held in her mouth and walked around to the other side. The seams had to be taken in evenly or the bodice would pucker instead of smoothly hugging Dedrah's slender curves. She repeated the procedure, gathering the fabric between the fingers of one hand, then smoothing the lines with the other before approaching with the pin. Dedrah trembled noticeably, and Layne let her hands fall away, exasperated. She snatched the pins from her mouth and inserted them in the cushion she wore at her wrist.

"Will you relax," she said for the third time. Then she added in a light tone, "I don't make pincushions of my clients, you know. It's bad for business."

Dedrah sighed heavily once more. "I'm sorry. I guess I'm just nervous."

"I guess you are," Layne agreed dryly. "Want to tell me why?"

Dedrah bit her lip, eyes downcast, then lifted a shoulder in a halfhearted shrug. "They're so stubborn," she said. "Once they make up their minds to something, that's it. I just don't know what to do with either one of them!" She threw her hands up, completely misaligning the hang of the bodice.

Layne tugged the dress back into place. She didn't have to ask of whom Dedrah was speaking. Who else but Rod and Sam Corley? Without question they were both stubborn, but they were unusually caring men, too, a fact of which she was certain she didn't have to remind Dedrah. So what, then, was the problem? She dismissed the fact that it might not be any of her business and put on a reassuring smile. "Want to tell me about it?"

Dedrah chewed her lip, then lifted pleading eyes to Layne. "I don't know if I should, you being so close to Rod and all."

Layne felt a surge of pleasure. So the family considered her close to Rod, did they? She hoped they were right. Then again, she didn't want to be in a position of having to take sides. It wasn't just that Sam and Dedrah were her clients, she hoped they were all going to be friends. Surely she could be "close" to Rod and Sam and Dedrah, too. Maybe now was the time to build that particular bridge. She unpinned the front of the dress and slipped it off Dedrah, then slung a pale pink robe over the girl's bare shoulders.

"Let's sit down," she said, indicating the chairs placed side by side before the mirror. Dedrah nodded and eased into one. Layne placed the unfinished dress on a hanger and came to sit beside her. She took Dedrah's hand in hers. It was cold and small. "Dedrah," she said, "I am very fond of Rod, and we have grown closer over the past several weeks, but I want you to know that I'm not in the habit of breaking confidences—not yours, not Rod's, not anyone's."

The girl smiled and squeezed Layne's hand. "It's that he won't tell him," she said, sighing.

"Sam, you mean?" Layne prodded gently. "What is it Sam won't tell Rod?"

Dedrah took a deep breath. "It's the wedding," she divulged quickly. "No offense, Miss Harington, but we'd rather not go through with it. We don't want to wait anymore, and we don't want all this bother and expense. We just want a quiet little ceremony with the family, but Sam won't tell Rod because he doesn't want to hurt him. Rod thinks it's best, you see. He has this thing about pride and putting on the best face and tripping up the gossips."

"He said something to me about this," Layne admitted thoughtfully. "You must know he's trying to protect Sam." But if they didn't want the wedding ... She shook her head, thinking how two well-intentioned but stubborn males could mess up the simplest things. Sam was keeping mum to spare Rod, and Rod, too, had his secrets designed to protect his nephew. How much better if they each explained themselves honestly. She wished she hadn't asked Dedrah to share her confidence, for now she, too, was pledged to keep silent. She put thumb and little finger to her temples and squeezed gently. It couldn't go on, but what was she to do? She couldn't very well counsel them herself. She was much too close to the situation for that. Counsel ... A switch flipped in her mind. "Dedrah," she began carefully, "would you mind if I shared this with the Reverend Charles? I assure you he would be very discreet, and I think he might advise Sam not only to tell Rod how he feels but how to go about it."

Dedrah cocked her head doubtfully. "I don't know. Sam might be upset with me for telling you, then letting you tell someone else...."

"But you're going to be honest with him about this, aren't you?" Layne urged. "Spouses shouldn't have secrets from one another, Dedrah. For the sake of your marriage alone, you have to tell him we've spoken."

Dedrah looked troubled. "I suppose you're right."

"Reverend Charles would want to counsel the two of you anyway, you know, and he's bound by ethics to keep the confidences of those who come to him for advice. I promise you he'll handle it delicately, and he just might have a solution for you. Please, let me call him."

"You don't mind," Dedrah asked, "that we might cancel all the plans you've made?"

Layne shook her head. At any other time, with anyone else, she might mind a good deal, but this situation was different—and personal. "I think honesty is always the best policy," she said, "especially among friends."

Dedrah clutched her hand tightly. "All right," she said breathlessly. "Call him. And I'll talk to Sam tonight."

Layne put her arms around the girl's shoulders. "I'm going to ask the reverend to keep me informed since we may be canceling the wedding. Is that all right with you?"

Dedrah shrugged and nodded. "Yeah, I guess so, as long as Sam agrees."

Layne hugged her. "Thanks, and don't worry. It's going to work out fine," she said. "You'll see."

Dedrah nodded, then her face brightened. "Can I get dressed now?" she asked. "Or do you want to stick more pins in me?"

Layne laughed and hugged her again. "You might as well get dressed," she said, then added teasingly, "I can always make a pincushion of you another time."

Dedrah giggled and went to reclaim her clothes, leaving Layne to wonder just how much she should tell Bolton Charles and if Rod would thank her for her interference.

It was late in the day before she had an opportunity to make a truly private phone call, and she feared the Reverend Mr. Charles would already have left his office for his home, but to her surprise, he answered the phone himself, his deep voice somehow bright.

"First Church of Duncan."

"Reverend Charles, I'm so glad I caught you in. This is Layne Harington."

"Layne! How nice to hear from you again. Sending another wedding our way so soon?"

"In fact, it has to do with the wedding we just scheduled."

"March/Corley?"

"That's right."

"How can I help?"

Was he psychic, she wondered, or just especially suited to his calling? A feeling of confidence stole over her. She had called the right person. She was doing the right thing. She took a deep breath and began. Several minutes later, she had reached the core of the problem.

"So you see, we've planned a wedding here that neither the bride nor the groom wants, but Sammy won't tell his uncle that because he doesn't want to hurt Rod's feelings. Of course, Rod is producing this gala affair in the first place because he wants to protect Sammy by helping him face down the critics and gossips out there. I guess his philosophy is similar to that of a strong offense being the best defense. Subconsciously he may even be hoping people will assume Sammy is *not* Heather's father, that he came into the picture after the fact—an idea that offends Sam. And Rod wouldn't stand still for it himself if he was in Sammy's shoes, but he's protected Sammy so long, it's just become second nature to him.''

"I certainly think that's understandable," Bolton Charles said. "Rod may be Sammy's uncle, but essentially he's the boy's parent, too. Obviously, he loves Sammy a great deal."

"That's exactly why he's kept certain information from Sammy all these years," Layne went on. "Things about his parents and his own birth, things even about his life with Rod. But now Sam's doing the same thing with him, and it's so unnecessary. They're two stubborn men bent on protecting one another, and somebody's got to do something about it. Somebody's got to help Sammy understand how to deal with his uncle."

"And you think I should be involved in that?" Bolton Charles asked.

"I was hoping you'd talk to Sammy, I mean, since you'd be doing a prewedding counseling session with him and Dedrah anyway."

"I'll be glad to speak to Sammy about this if Sammy wants to speak to me."

"Dedrah's arranging that," Layne told him. "I thought we could just schedule a counseling session as if it were the standard prewedding consultation. Then we can see what happens when they get there."

"All right. If Sam or Dedrah brings up their dissatisfaction with the wedding you and Rod have planned, I'll be prepared to discuss it with them. Shall we make the appointment now?"

"Please, and I'll pass on the day and time to Dedrah."

"Fine. Just let me get the appointment book from my secretary's desk." Layne waited until he returned some moments later, then they set a late afternoon appointment for early the next week. "Now," he said, changing his tone, "is there anything I can do for *you.*"

Layne smiled. Not only was the Reverend Bolton Charles a very caring man, extremely personable, eager to help all who came to him, he was devastatingly handsome—and absolutely mad about his wife, a particular friend of Layne's. Much more for his devotion than his looks, Layne liked him immensely and respected him even more. "Thank you, Bolton," she said, reverting to his given name now that the conversation had taken on a more personal tone, "but besides keeping me informed, I can't think of anything. I'm fine."

"Good to know that," he said, "but if an old friend is allowed an observation, you seem more involved with your clients than usual."

She laughed silently. Bolton *was* psychic. She sat forward, bracing her elbow on the desktop. "I've been dating Rod Corley for some time now," she divulged congenially, "and I'd like to go on doing so."

"Ah-ha. I smell a romance. Any chance you'll be planning your own wedding before long?"

Layne frowned. She didn't want to think about that, didn't want to weigh the chances. "We're a long way from anything like that," she said carefully. "We've both been on the shelf a long time. Rod's been on the shelf even longer than I have. Forty years old and never been married. I don't think marriage is a priority with either of us."

"Love has a way of changing priorities," Bolton said gently.

She closed her eyes, tamping down the unbidden flare of hope. "Nobody's mentioned the 'L-word,' Bolton," she said, "but if and when we get around to it, I'll be sure to let you and Carol know."

He chuckled. "You do that. Carol will be on pins and needles until she hears."

Layne grinned, knowing her old college chum was one of the last great romantics. She could see the stars in Carol's eyes now. "Tell her I'll stop by and fill her in myself. This is prime girl talk."

"She'd like that, Layne," he said, "especially now." Something in the tone of his voice made her tighten her grip on the telephone receiver.

"Bolton, is something wrong?"

He paused. She could almost hear him deciding how much to say. "It's a health issue," he finally revealed. "We decided it was past time to get serious about having a baby, but it turns out there are problems."

Layne grimaced at the wall. "I'm so sorry to hear that. Is there anything I can do?"

"We welcome all prayers," he said, then some of his usual good cheer seemed to reassert itself, and he added, "and rumors of romance."

She laughed outright. "Glad to have been of some service then!"

"Always a pleasure to hear from you," he said. "I'll tell Carol to expect you."

"Do that," she replied, "and, Reverend, thanks."

"Anytime, Layne, anytime at all."

They hung up, and for a moment she sat staring at the phone. Poor Carol. She and Layne were the very same age, but while Layne had been caught up in her studies at the university, Carol had been dropping out to marry a charming young minister from the western portion of the state. Layne remembered Carol's quiet joy and the sparkle in her eye when she'd spoken about having a family with the man of her dreams. How sad that that particular joy might be denied her.

Layne knew suddenly that her empathy for Carol Charles's situation was greatly enhanced by her own feelings for Rod Corley. If sweet, good Carol's dreams could not come true, how much less likely were her own? It was then that Layne did something she had never done before. She picked up the phone again and called Rod Corley with a purely personal message. If he would like to join her, she would be delighted to make dinner for him that evening.

He would, and she did, and the kiss they shared upon parting was long and lingering and completely proper.

When the day of the appointment rolled around, Layne was rather uneasy to see that Rod had come along with Sam and Dedrah. He walked into the shop with Heather seated in the fold of one arm, grinned at Layne as if publicly divulging a secret shared only by the two of them and bent to kiss her cheek. Dedrah schooled a quick smile, Heather grabbed a handful of Layne's sleek chestnut hair and Angie gasped from the window where she was arranging a new display of winter wedding finery.

"Coming with us, aren't you?" Rod asked in that deep, soft voice of his. "Heather and I are counting on your company."

She had intended to lead the way for Sam and Dedrah, introduce them to Bolton Charles, then drive her own car back here to work, but she abandoned that idea instantly and gave an affirmative reply to Rod's question. Within two minutes, she and Rod were driving toward the First Church in her car, Sam, Dedrah and Heather following in Rod's truck. Ten minutes after that, they were walking up a gently curving concrete path toward the First Church of Duncan.

She loved this church and its stately, traditional architecture. Dark red brick gave the building an air of solidity and permanence, while the tall, white, elaborately molded double doors spoke of welcome and acceptance. A steep, green roof of many peaks and angles rose toward the heavens, the tall white steeple atop the bell tower leading the way, while beneath the eaves and behind gracefully arched porticoes stained-glass Gothic windows glowed richly. The grounds were lovingly maintained, the gardener having managed to coax a pale but verdant green from the thick grass even in these first weeks of winter. Low, sculpted shrubs hugged the ground close to the building. A number of mature pecan trees graced the lawn, though their limbs were bare and spindly against the gray sky. Nestled among them were a few thick, conical cedars, each identical to the others, thanks to meticulous pruning. Upon the ground lay not a single twig, leaf, nut, stone, needle or fragment of bark. The whole of it was as pristine as a painting, and Layne never failed to find a sense of peace here, as if she were walking upon truly hallowed ground.

Rod walked beside her, Heather against his shoulder, looking backward. Sam and Dedrah followed, hands linked. All were quiet, as if moved to silence by the place where they walked. Layne led them past the sanctuary doors, down the covered portico and around the corner to an unprepossessing portal set above a single, broad step. Above it hung a small sign suspended by two lengths of chain. It read simply, Office. An even smaller sign bolted to the door just above the knob bade them welcome and listed three telephone numbers to be called in case of an emergency. Layne opened the door and stepped into a small room lincd with chairs. An octagon of colored light spilled onto the wood floor from a small window set high in one corner. The door to the next room stood open, and Layne walked through it, leaving the others behind to settle themselves awkwardly in chairs.

Sitting behind the desk in the small, closetlike office was not the older, matronly woman Layne expected to find, but Carol Charles herself. "Layne!" she cried excitedly, her pale oval face lighting with a smile. Layne was rocked to the very core of her being, not by the greeting, which was perfectly consistent with every other she'd ever received from the gentle, gracious woman, but by the ghastly pallor and thinning hair of the seriously ill. For a sharp instant, Layne could neither respond nor contain her rioting emotions, but then sheer fondness prevailed, and she felt her stiffened facial muscles relax into a semblance of a smile.

"Carol," she said, forcing every shred of gladness she could find into her voice. "How delighted I am to see you."

"Bolt told me you were coming, and as our secretary is on vacation just now, I thought I'd come down and fill in. How are you?"

Better than you, dear Carol, Layne answered silently, and something of her thoughts must have communicated themselves, for Carol's smile grew suddenly wistful.

"He didn't prepare you very well, did he? But I'm sure it's as much my fault as his. You know how I am, I can't bear having a fuss made over me, and we are optimistic. Faith can conquer even cancer, you know."

Cancer. The word clanged against Layne's eardrums like the cymbal of doom. "Oh, Carol," she said, abandoning stoicism. Impulsively she leaned over the desk and wrapped her arms around the other woman's neck, feeling every delicate bone. She caught the sob that built in her chest just in time and managed to ask, "Is there anything I can do?"

Amazingly, Carol laughed. "I think we'll leave it to God and the doctors, but never mind that. I hear you and I have much to discuss."

Layne gave up the hug and blinked away tears. "I'd like you to meet someone," she said softly, and stepping to the door, she motioned the others to join her. They crowded into the small office, Rod seeming to fill every corner all by himself. "This is Rod Corley," she said, placing a hand on his forearm. "This is his nephew, Sammy, and this—" she dropped a hand onto Dedrah's shoulder "—is our bride-to-be, Dedrah March, with her darling daughter, Heather."

Carol didn't bat an eyelash as she rose smoothly to her feet, bestowed smiles on all, and brushed fingertips wistfully over Heather's fine, light brown hair. Secure, loved and unaware of danger in the world, Heather reached out for this gentle, but unknown lady.

"Oh, may I?" Carol asked hopefully, and Dedrah placed the wriggling child in her arms. Heather immediately stilled, stuck her hand in her mouth and babbled around it confidently. "What a charmer," Carol cooed. "Such a beauty, and so loving!"

As if to prove her praise, Heather flung a moist hand around Carol's neck and laid her head on Carol's shoulder. Carol laughed delightedly, and it was then that the door to the inner office opened and the Reverend Bolton Charles beamed down on them all.

He was the kind of handsome that made female hearts flutter. In his mid-thirties, dark of hair and eye, tall and lean and broad of shoulder, he had the face of a movie star and beneath the well-fitted suit and stark white shirt, the body of an athlete. "I think my substitute secretary would keep you all to herself if I'd let her," he said amiably, "but I'm not about to. Layne, it's good to see you." He briefly grasped both of her hands in his, then dropped them and turned to greet her companions. He shook each hand in turn as the introductions were made, even the baby's, who, sensing a new receptor for her particular brand of enchantment, lifted her head and bestowed a wet, gurgling smile.

"An angel!" Bolton Charles announced to the gathering in general, rubbing a hand across her little back. "Yes, I believe I feel the stubs of tiny wings now."

Everyone laughed, Heather joining in belatedly and without the slightest idea why, knowing only that she was once more the center of attention. Suddenly she spied her uncle Rod and launched herself at him, arms outflung in total trust. He caught her up and folded her safely against his chest, whereupon she grabbed hold of the point of his shirt collar and mangled it in her small fist.

"Well, we know who the favorite is," Bolton said complacently.

"Now that's a fact," Sammy said, "except when her grandpa is around. Her grandpa March thinks the sun rises and shines for his Heather."

"Doesn't it?" Rod asked, and everyone laughed again.

"Got a point there," Sammy admitted proudly.

The reverend gave them his most laudatory smile. "Children should be adored," he said, fixing his seal of approval upon them all. "Sam, Dedrah, if you're ready, I'll speak with you now."

"We'll take care of Heather," Rod said, and as he did so, his free arm drifted down and around Layne's shoulder, leaving no doubt about whom was included in "we."

Carol smiled like the cat who'd swallowed the canary, clasped her hands behind her and rocked up on her toes. Layne could not help and did not try to prevent the flush of pleasure that came over her, but neither was she willing to stand there and let Carol drool over them as though they were particularly sweet chocolates in a heart-shaped box. One more small and probably meaningless gesture from Rod like the last one and Carol would be asking if they were ready to set a wedding date. Better she talk to Carol about Rod in private and vice versa. That being the case, she came up with a brilliant idea. Luckily the weather was clear and crisp and still.

"Why don't we put Heather's coat on her and take her out to the playground?"

"Good idea," Rod answered agreeably, and then retreated into the waiting room to stuff Heather's little limbs into pink insulated sleeves.

Layne shot a look at Carol, hoping to convey that though she wanted to visit with her old friend, duty called her elsewhere at the moment. Carol was not fooled, nor was she wounded. Grinning, she pointed at Rod's retreating back, then formed a circle with her thumb and forefinger. The message was unmistakable: Carol approved of Layne's choice in men. It was all Layne could do not to laugh aloud. As it was, she snickered, then feigned a sneeze when Rod glanced back over his shoulder. Carol's light voice pealed forth, however, and Layne marveled that so gay and happy a sound could come from a woman whose hopes of bearing her own children had been dashed and replaced with the specter of cancer. Surely it wasn't life-threatening. No, she decided, it couldn't be, and adoption was always a possibility. That thought made her feel better, and she left her friend with a smile.

Layne and Rod walked through the maze of porticoes and covered walkways at a leisurely pace. They were in no hurry, and though the weather was crisp, it was not uncomfortable as long as they were bundled into their coats and kept moving. Heather's mittens were in place, and her hood had been drawn up over her dainty ears, its strings tied snugly beneath her perpetually moist chin. The church grounds were working their particular magic, making words unnecessary and silence companionable, so it wasn't until they reached the playground that Rod attempted conversation.

"You were right," he said, after seating Heather into a safety swing and giving her a little push.

"That's nice. What was I right about?"

"About the reverend and his wife. You said I'd like them, and I do."

"They're very special people," she commented, thinking again how unfair it was that Carol, sweet and kind as she was, should be fighting cancer when she wanted to be having babies. The weight of his hand on her shoulder surprised her. She switched her gaze abruptly and found herself staring up into soft, gray-blue eyes.

"Is something wrong?"

"No, not with me. Why?"

"You seem sad."

Layne shrugged and looked down at Heather, who was leaning forward in the gently swaying swing as if she could make it go faster by sheer force of will. For some reason, she didn't want to tell Rod about Carol Charles's trouble. "I was just thinking that you'd make a great father," she said.

Rod sent her a sharp but not necessarily displeased look. "Now what brought that up?"

She laughed. "I don't know. Heather, I guess. She sure charmed the Charleses, didn't she?"

"She did that. Now they'd be great parents, both of them."

Layne nodded, feeling sad for them again. "Yes, they would," she agreed softly.

Rod smiled at her, and with one hand he reached out and pushed Heather a little higher. The other he sent across Layne's shoulders to pull her close to his side.

A feeling of warmth and well-being suffused Layne. Was he thinking about the kind of parents the Charleses would be, or was he thinking about the kind of parents the two of them would make? She pondered that, she and Rod with a child of their own. What a lovely picture. As if in protest Heather started to fuss. Sounds of distress emitted from her open mouth, while her back arched and her arms reached upward. Rod responded at once.

"What's the matter, pumpkin? Bored already?" He plucked her up out of the bucket of the swing, fished a handkerchief out of his back pocket and wiped her nose and chin. "Want to try the bouncing elephant?" He carried her over to a small blue elephant mounted on a large steel spring. Carefully he seated her, tucked her tiny feet into the metal stirrups, curled her teeny hands around the metal handles and, holding her in place, rocked the elephant up and down and side to side. Heather squealed and attempted to stand in the stirrups, bouncing herself about twice as fast as Rod moved the elephant.

Layne laughed. Oh, yes, this man definitely ought to have children of his own. What a wonderful father he would be, every bit as capable and loving as Bolton Charles. She closed her eyes and said a silent prayer for Carol and Bolton.

Half an hour later, they had worked their way through three more spring set animals, a seesaw, a slide, and the merry-go-round. Bolton appeared at the top of the yard and signaled them to return to the church building. Heather's cheeks were pink and her nose was running, but she was in high spirits, babbling and cooing and clapping her hands as Rod lifted her against his shoulder and they started back the way they'd come. Bolton didn't wait for them, but moved in out of the chill and was sitting with the others, chatting amiably when Layne, Rod and Heather strolled in.

They stayed long enough for Dedrah to change Heather's diaper, a process the little one found highly objectionable. Everyone seemed quite relaxed and friendly, with no hint of how the conversation between Sam, Dedrah and the reverend had progressed. At last, they all rose to go. Heather was cajoled into giving Carol a messy kiss on the cheek. The reverend settled for a finger shake, his index finger gripped tightly by Heather's now grimy fist. Layne promised Carol that she would visit soon and received Carol's pleased, serene smile in return.

They began to leave. Dedrah, with Heather, led the way. Sam and Rod followed. Then just before Layne stepped through the door, Bolton dropped a hand upon her shoulder.

"May I call you later?" he asked softly. "It was agreed that I could discuss certain matters with you."

"Please do," she answered quickly. He smiled reassuringly and released her. She stepped out and closed the door, glimpsing the Reverend Bolton Charles as he took his ailing wife into his arms. *They'll be all right,* she told herself. They simply had to be.

Seized by a sense of urgency, she hurried to catch up with the others, suddenly needing some sort of connection with those dear to her. When she slipped her hand into Rod's, he smiled down at her, linked his fingers through hers, and carried them into his coat pocket, where they felt safe and warm. She and Rod would be all right, too, no matter what happened with Sam and Dedrah and the wedding. They had to be.

Chapter Seven

Rev. Bolton Charles called that evening. He was positive and upbeat and chatty, and he didn't want her to worry. Sammy Corley and Dedrah March were credible young people, very much in love and dealing with a difficult situation as best they could, a situation for which each felt a certain guilt. Nevertheless, they loved their angelic little girl fiercely and proudly. They wanted to provide her with a secure, happy home, and they wanted to do it right away, but Sammy especially was committed to honoring his uncle's wishes in the matter, wrongheaded as he thought them to be. Rev. Bolton Charles, for his part, found no objection with Rod Corley's plans for his nephew and niece-to-be. They were, of course, entitled to make their own plans, but so long as they were committed to Rod's, however unhappily, the reverend saw no reason for Layne to be overly concerned. The reverend's advice to her was that she do the job for which she was hired and keep an ear open and a shoulder at the ready for Dedrah, should the girl need them. Meanwhile, he would continue to counsel Sam and Dedrah as he would any other couple about to marry.

His manner and comments made Layne feel better. She still considered the wedding she was planning to be unnecessary as Dedrah and Sam did not want it, but if they were determined to go along with it, she would plan them a wedding to make them and Rod proud. That settled in her mind, she changed the subject to Carol's health.

Hearing that things were not going well, she said, "I'm so sorry, Bolton. Carol's the last person something like this should happen to."

"It's not a punishment, Layne," he told her soothingly. "For all that it is a tragedy, it's not a punishment, and why shouldn't we be touched by tragedy as much as anyone else? No one ever promised us an untroubled life on this planet, only that God would give us the strength and ability to cope with whatever comes. That being the case, you might say we're optimistically resigned to our fate."

"You aren't afraid for her then?"

"Of course I'm afraid for her," he said. "I'm afraid for me. I'm afraid for everyone who loves Carol, but we have much to encourage us. I won't be morose, and I don't want anyone else to be. Carol would hate that."

For some reason that heartened her. "All right. We'll apply our faith, and allow God to do what He does best."

"Amen to that," he said, the smile in his voice somehow audible, "and thank you."

"Thank *you*," she said by way of farewell and hung up.

Life was almost too normal. Business was good, Rod was attentive, Dedrah was shy and Sam was silent.

Heather, however, was obviously growing fond of "Miss Layne", taking it for granted that Miss Layne was equally fond of her, which she was, of course. More and more often, Layne found herself going over details of the March/Corley wedding with Heather in her lap. The child sat, gnawing on the ends of pencils, drooling on papers, thrashing and babbling and just generally being the darling babe that she was. If that particular turn of events also meant that Layne spent a good deal of time removing milk and apple juice from her clothing, she considered it inconsequential. But even more important were the silent looks of approval that Rod gave her whenever she took Heather in hand. Layne had come to believe with all her heart that he and she should have children together. What they had, however, was a date to the Cattleman's Ball.

The Cattleman's Association annual dinner dance was the social event of the year, and when he invited her, Rod admitted that he had never attended before. He was not, he said, one for socializing with large groups of people, most of whom where strangers, but he felt he ought to make an exception this year, especially as the prettiest woman in town would be on his arm. She went to work right away trying to live up to that description.

The dress she made for the occasion was stunning. A dark green satin formed the strapless, fitted bodice, and the tulip overskirt split in front to reveal a tea-length underskirt. A short, long-sleeved jacket with a wedding ring collar was made from the same flowered satin as the underskirt. She had satin heels dyed to match the forest green and ordered stockings to match.

For the evening, she swept her dark chestnut hair into a sleek, sophisticated French roll on the back of her head, clipped enormous emerald green glass jewels onto her

dainty earlobes, and hung a matching necklace around
her slender neck. Her grandmother's rhinestone brace-
let, circa 1930, went around her wrist, and the small emerald pin her parents had given her as a graduation gift
became a hair ornament tucked into the seam at the back
of her head.

All in all, she was pleased with her appearance but
nervous, nonetheless. Then she opened the front door of
the shop, the agreed meeting place, and Rod's face lit up
like a light bulb. All her doubts fled, and she laughed in
sheer delight. He was no slouch, either, dressed in a well-
tailored black suit of a modified Western cut, a white
shirt with a tucked front and French cuffs, a black silk tie
with a single red stripe angled diagonally and black dress
boots with low heels and rounded toes. His tie clip was a
narrow gold bar with a tiny ruby set in its center, a gold
watch his only other jewelry. Layne thought him the most
handsome man she'd ever seen, and she decided without
vanity or self-service that they made a very attractive
couple.

She was right. Every eye that met hers when they entered the hotel ballroom told her so. Rod had said that
most of those present would be strangers, but it seemed
to Layne that nearly everyone knew him. Certainly, lots
of hands lifted in greeting, and more than one beckoned
them over for an exchange of pleasantries. Rod, however, had reserved a private table for them, and Layne
was not displeased. She really didn't want to share him
with anyone tonight. Neither did she mind that they sat
out most of the dances. Rod, by his own admission, was
woefully inexperienced on the dance floor, and she determined privately to correct that at first opportunity. It
would be fun to move back the living room furniture, put
on a compact disc and instruct him in the privacy of her

own home. They would laugh and dance and kiss and plan an evening out when they would put every other couple on the dance floor to shame. But for now, she was happy just to sit at the table with him, eat, talk, laugh and know that she was the envy of every other woman in the room.

It was late when Rod decided that he wanted to walk out for a breath of fresh air. She suggested they get their coats, but he promised he would keep her warm, saying they'd stay out of the reach of the cold winter wind. His eyes seemed to promise another kind of protection, and her heart sped up at the thought of standing with his arms about her, his mouth on hers. They slipped out a side door and hurried around the corner to escape the bite of the breeze. There her hopes materialized as he pulled her into his arms and kissed her hungrily, his lips and tongue telling her more accurately than words ever could what the sight of her in that dress was doing to him. She, too, had a message to send. She was his and his alone, ready and willing to acknowledge that fact whenever he decided the time was right. It seemed to her, as that kiss heated and branded, that the time was close at hand. They were standing there in the deep, cold shadows, warming each other with passion when voices and the scuffle of feet told them these moments of privacy were at an end.

"Damned wind," complained one, and the other chuckled. "Hard to have a smoke in the wind."

"Hard to have a smoke anywhere these days," said his friend, and they both paused to drag on their cigarettes, the tips glowing red in the dark.

Rod tucked her head beneath his chin and tightened his arms about her, very silent, lest they be discovered trysting in the shadows. Layne smiled against his shirtfront and snuggled contentedly into the warmth of his body inside his suit jacket. The two men continued talking, one complaining about the dinner service, the other about his wife's lack of tact in dealing with the recalcitrant waitress. "Cute little thing, that waitress," he muttered suggestively.

"I was too busy looking at Corley's date to notice," said the other, and Layne's head jerked back as Rod's chest rose sharply beneath her cheek.

"Who is she?" came the question.

"I don't know. My wife said something about a wedding service. One thing's for sure, though, she's too good for a Corley."

Rod stiffened at that, and Layne placed a hand against his chest, hoping he wouldn't give them away.

"Why do you say that?" one fellow was asking, and the other snorted derisively.

"His old man was a common criminal. Died in the pen. And his brother would have ended up the same way if he hadn't killed himself driving drunk. His kid doesn't look to be much different, either. He apparently knocked up Able March's daughter last year."

Layne gasped, and the next instant Rod had thrust her away. For one wild second she thought he was going to challenge those two men there in the dark, but then he grabbed her hand and hauled her off in the opposite direction. Behind them, the two men tossed their cigarette stubs into the wind and wondered aloud who or what was going there. Layne bit her lip. Rod's father had been a common criminal. How that must have hurt him! They rounded the corner into the light, the wind flailing them with its icy touch. Rod's face was set in hard, bitter lines, and she longed to reach out to him, soothe him with her words, but talking was useless in this cold, sharp wind.

He pulled her through the front door of the building, scraped his hand through his wind-tousled hair and informed her he was getting their coats then strode away.

With shaking hands, she patted her own hair into place, wondering how deeply that overheard bit of venom had struck. Other thoughts came unbidden, too. Had Rod's father really been a criminal? If so, how could such a man have produced so fine a son as Rod? And what of his mother? What had happened to her?

Rod came back almost immediately to shove her coat onto her shoulders and herd her back out into the wind. They drove to her house in near silence, her futile attempts at discussion rebuffed without comment or glance. In her front drive, he put the vehicle in Park but did not shut off the engine. The face he turned to her was cold and implacable, but she sensed a vulnerability and wounding that ran dangerously deep.

"I'm sorry you had to hear that," he said thickly, and she hastened to correct him, her head shaking as her hand went out to touch his wrist.

"What those two said doesn't mean anything to me."

His gaze, sad beyond endurance, locked onto her fingers where they lay upon his wrist. "It should," he said softly. "They'll be tarring and feathering you with the same brush next, and once they begin, it won't matter how hard you work or how high your morals, they'll keep right on and never stop."

"You can't let such small-minded people get to you, Rod," she argued gently. "No one cares what people like that have to say."

"Yes, they do," he replied sadly. "Your mama will care. Your daddy will care. Everybody who loves you will care once those small-minded people blacken your name, too. They'll care, and they'll blame me—and rightly so."

"That's just not true, Rod," she vowed, but he shook his head morosely.

"It's true. I know because it's happened before." He whacked a fist against the steering wheel, suddenly angry. "I should have known! I should have known!"

Frightened, she tightened her grip on his wrist, entreating him. "Come inside, Rod, and let's talk this out. We can talk it through, put it into perspective."

He twisted free of her with pitifully little effort. "I can't come in," he said. "Don't ask me to."

"Please, Rod—"

"I won't have your name linked with mine after this! I don't know what I was thinking of, what I expected! It's always been like this, Layne. I just don't usually hear it said straight out. Maybe it's a good thing I did, so I can stop this before it's too late."

"Don't say that. I don't want to stop anything between us."

"It's already stopped."

"No, it isn't! I have a say in this, you know."

He sighed and pressed a hand to his forehead. "Not anymore. Now go in the house, Layne."

"Not until—"

"Go in the house!"

"Rod—"

"I mean it, Layne! Go in the house!"

She stared at him, mouth ajar, for a long time. Obviously he meant it. He'd made up his mind, and nothing she could say was going to change it—for now. She pulled a deep breath, steeled herself and nodded sharply.

"All right, I'll go in, but I'm not through with you, Rod Corley, and you're not through with me, whatever you may think!" She yanked the door handle and slid out onto the ground. Turning, she closed the door gently and backed away.

He put the truck in Reverse and backed it out of the drive. He came to a halt in the street. The truck engine rumbled smoothly, and the cold wind whipped around her, tearing at her hair, plastering her coat to her back and ruffling her skirts. She felt his gaze, longing, regretful; then the truck lurched slightly and rolled forward. Layne held her skirts down and watched him drive away, as cold inside as out.

Christmas came and went. Layne called and left messages on his answering machine, but he didn't return them. If it was business, something to do with the wedding, then Dedrah or Sammy called with confused apologies and a message for relay, but none of her subtle attempts to reach Rod yielded results. Then, the last week in January, he walked into the shop with Dedrah and Heather. His scowl told her that he was not happy to be there, but despite that and the pounding of her heart, she smiled and managed to conduct business. She had been after Dedrah for some time to choose colors so that dresses and decorations could be ordered, and at last Dedrah was here to comply. With serenity she was far from feeling, Layne ushered the trio into the consultation room, seated them at the table and took her own chair, opening the notebook Dedrah had given her.

"Have you decided colors?"

Dedrah nodded. "I think so, peach and green, kind of a pale, silvery, spring green."

Coolly, Layne flipped open a sample book. "Can you find it here?"

For several minutes, Dedrah studied sample after sample of fabric swatches, occasionally nudging Rod for an opinion. "This?" she would ask. "Maybe this?"

He kept his attention on Heather and his answers invariably short and snappish. For once, he had no opinion, no preference, no interest. Layne wondered why he had come. To see her, perhaps? Hope sped her heartbeat, but as time passed and he did not look at her, did not directly answer her few contrived questions, did not give her one sign that he regretted his decision made the night of the Cattleman's Ball, hope languished and reality set in. He actually meant to stay apart from her.

How could it be over between them just because a couple of faceless voices in the dark had chosen to gossip over cigarettes? What they had said was mean and ugly, and Rod undoubtedly thought he was protecting her, but the truth was that nothing had ever hurt her as deeply as losing him. How could she make him understand that?

The man was nothing if not stubborn. Once he made up his mind to something, that was that. But surely, if he loved her, he wouldn't let anything so superficial as gossip stand in their way, *if* he loved her. She could not bear to think that he did not return her feelings, but the thought was inescapable when he sat across the table from her jiggling the baby on his knee as if her heart was not breaking.

By the time they were finished for the day, Layne was so uptight her hands were visibly trembling and her shoulders felt as if the muscles were tied in knots. It was almost a relief when Rod pushed back his chair, hoisted Heather onto his shoulder, got up and walked out. Then again the sight of his retreating back evoked such a sense of loss in Layne that she very nearly called him back.

Only the fear that he would ignore her summons kept her tongue still and her mouth shut, but when the door closed behind him, tears welled into her eyes. She remembered Dedrah only when the girl's slender hand squeezed her forearm. Blinking rapidly, she switched her gaze to find a sympathetic smile trained upon her.

"He didn't tell us what happened," Dedrah said, "only that you aren't seeing each other anymore."

Layne looked away, the tears threatening to spill over onto her cheeks. She couldn't speak without further betraying herself, but what would she have said anyway? Unable to respond in any other way, she simply shook her head. The hand on her forearm tightened.

"If it's any consolation to you," Dedrah said quietly, "he's as unhappy as you are."

Knowing that *did* help. Layne swallowed down the tears and returned her gaze to Dedrah's piquant face. "I know he's only trying to do what he thinks is best," she said, her voice little more than a whisper, "but, Dedrah, I can't stand this. I have to find a way to change his mind."

Dedrah sighed. "Good luck," she said. "I wish I could help, but I don't know how."

Layne smiled tremulously. "Thanks anyway, but I guess no one can do anything really. I can't even get him to talk to me."

Dedrah nodded. "I know. Sam says we ought to lock you two into a closet together and not let you out until you've settled it."

"Just point me toward the closet," Layne quipped dryly. "Maybe the army will help him get Rod into it."

"Oh, there has to be a way," Dedrah said, ignoring the attempt at humor.

Suddenly, there was. Layne's eyes lit as she considered the idea that had so abruptly presented itself. Did she dare do it? She bit her lip, thinking. Why not? What did she have to lose? She seized Dedrah by the shoulders. "Did you mean it? Would you help me make Rod listen?"

Dedrah looked surprised, but her spine stiffened. "I meant it."

Layne hugged her, speaking swiftly. "Listen to me. It's time to decide the menu for the reception. I was going to call you soon and invite you to a buffet of sample dishes the hotel catering service offers. I'm still going to, and I want you and Sam to persuade Rod to come with you. Just don't tell him you won't be staying."

"All right," Dedrah agreed instantly, "but how will you get him to stay if we don't?"

"Let me worry about that," Layne said. "You just get him there, and let me worry about the rest. Can you do that?"

"Yes. Somehow."

Layne hugged her again. "Thank you so much."

Dedrah nodded, her eyes very large. "He's going to be awfully mad," she told Layne solemnly.

"Yes, he is," Layne conceded, "but I'll try to see to it that he isn't mad with you or Sam."

Dedrah shrugged pensively. "I'm afraid it's going to happen sooner or later anyway. Oh, Layne, I don't know if we can go through with this wedding. Sammy doesn't want to hurt Rod and neither do I, but we so want to marry quietly and simply—and soon."

"Then you have to tell Rod that," Layne counseled firmly. "Do it before the invitations go out, Dedrah. Please."

"I can't," she said. "Sammy would never forgive me."

"Then get Sammy to tell him."

"I'm not sure I can do that, either," Dedrah said. "Like Rod, his impulse is to protect those he loves, and no sacrifice is too great to accomplish that. Yet, the more time passes, the harder it gets to go along with this. Still, I can't put Sammy in the position of having to choose between what I want and what Rod wants."

"So everybody tries to protect everybody else and none of us is really happy," Layne summed up angrily.

"Not right now, but eventually," Dedrah argued gently. "Sam and I will get married one way or another, and you and Rod will get back together. I just know you will."

Layne slipped her arm about Dedrah's shoulders and turned her toward the door. "I hope you're right," she said. "I pray you're right."

Rod looked at his reflection in the mirror and prayed he wasn't making a mistake. It was so hard to see her, harder than he'd realized it would be. And yet, in all the years he'd held himself apart from others, he'd never wanted to see anyone else so badly. That knowledge revealed the lie in the pride he'd felt at holding himself apart all his life. Oh, he'd fancied himself in love once or twice before, but somehow those feelings had changed rather quickly. He couldn't really put his finger on what had happened, but he'd always suspected that the gossip about his family was behind it. Never before had that suspicion been confirmed, however. Now he knew that he had no right to taint another with the Corley reputation, certainly not Layne. She was too fine for that. Of course, she didn't understand. How could she? Only one who had found himself the object of such gossip could know how deeply it hurt to be talked about disparagingly. He remembered all too well the very first time he'd heard the talk that swirled around the Corley name.

Second grade was an impressionable time for a child, and Rod had liked school especially well that year, at least in the beginning. Since his mother had drunk herself into an early grave, he'd been in dire need of nurturing, and his teacher, Miss Kinsale, seemed to have recognized that he was neglected. He had been so proud to be "teacher's pet" and had eagerly passed out papers, cleaned erasers, sharpened pencils and carried messages. He had, in fact, done any- and everything she had asked of him, and it was in returning from an errand she had assigned him, one that had claimed the majority of his recess time, that he had chanced to overhear the remarks his teacher had made to another.

"I just hope it will have some impact," she had said. "I know the Corleys are no good, but Rod is just a child and kindness can work wonders. Of course, I can't trust him with the milk money or anything like that, but I can show him the benefits of hard work."

Rod had never known what reply the other teacher had made. The pain had roared through him with deafening intensity. Miss Kinsale did not trust him. The Corleys were no good. He had turned and run, leaving the school grounds and trudging the long way home, only to arrive and find that, though the school day was finished and the bus had already run, he hadn't been missed at all. Neither had anyone noticed that he'd stayed home the next day. His father and older brother had seemed to be consumed by their own interests. Eventually, however, Miss Kinsale had driven out to his house to ask why he had stopped attending school. His father had laughed and asked if he'd played hooky from school. When Rod hadn't answered, Barry had gloatingly informed their father that Rod hadn't been on the bus either the past two afternoons or that morning, either. Duke Corley had then backhanded Rod, knocking him to the floor.

Miss Kinsale had been appalled and upbraided his father for knocking him down, but Duke Corley had loudly proclaimed that nobody told him what to do, least of all some uptight, do-gooder teacher. To that, Miss Kinsale had declared, "No wonder your sons are not to be trusted!" She had then turned and stomped out of the house. Rod had silently vowed in that very moment that he would, indeed, prove himself trustworthy, but not for Miss Kinsale, never for the teacher who had disillusioned him so.

Miss Kinsale had referred to what had happened that day only once and then to explain why he would have no opportunity to make up missed work. "I don't approve of what your father did," she had said, "but I don't approve of skipping school, either, and I am very hurt, Rod, that you took advantage of my trust to leave the school grounds. Because I had dispatched you on an errand, you knew I wouldn't look for you until well after recess was over, and by then it was too late. Because of that, I'm afraid I can't allow you to make up the work you've missed."

He had taken his unexcused absence—and the zeros in grade that had accompanied it—stoically. In the same way, he had endured the removal of Miss Kinsale's favor. No more errands had been assigned him, and he had volunteered for none. Because of Miss Kinsale he had known ever after what the whispers at his back were and why they were, but he remembered, too, that his own actions had cost him most. He had decided such would never be the case again, and as he got older, he had added to that rule. He had come to understand that he could never allow anyone else to suffer because of his behavior. He would not be one of those "no good" Corleys. No matter what the gossips said and no matter the hurt, his personal pride would not allow him to be careless in his actions or motives. Sadly, he had quickly seen that he could not defend his father and brother, but neither would he copy them, even though failure to do so had often caused him trouble at home, where his own parent and sibling had called him "coward" and "do-gooder" and even "wimp."

It had been a lonely life Rod Corley had laid out for himself, but he didn't regret the choices he had made, particularly where it came to Sammy. He and Sammy had been painted with the same brush, even before they came to live together, but Rod had been and remained determined that Sammy would never know the kind of hurt and loneliness he had known as a child—and even now.

Rod turned away from his image in the mirror, rejecting but not denying the loneliness and yearning he saw there. He had been foolish to think that his lifetime of honest labor could erase the cloud from his past and heritage. Too, he had made grave errors, some he couldn't even identify. Why else would Sammy have been so incircumspect and careless as to get Dedrah pregnant out of wedlock? Rod sighed. It was useless to ask such questions and worse than useless to blame Sam for that mistake. All he, Rod, could do was try to help, to protect the boy who had come to mean so much to him, as well as the others he loved—Dedrah, Heather, Layne. Layne.

He couldn't forgive himself for exposing her to the Corley taint. Why had he thought it "safe" to cultivate a relationship with Layne? He had known from the beginning that she was a woman above reproach, and a

woman like that had no business with a Corley. He was
no starry-eyed youth in the grip of strong emotion and
stronger desires for the first time. He was forty years old,
old enough to know better, and yet, what hopes he had
had for himself and Layne!

He supposed he should be glad that he'd taken her to
that blasted dinner dance. At least he'd been forced to
face what he had exposed her to. Still, he couldn't help
wishing that he'd been allowed to make his mistakes in
ignorance. Layne Harington was the dearest, most delicious, most decent woman he'd ever known. Just the idea
that she liked him, wanted to spend time with him, actually responded to him was enough to fill him with joy.
To have her company, her concern, her care was like
basking in a dream-come-true.

How could he give that up? But for her sake, he would.
For her sake, he would do anything, give up anything. He
loved her and he knew it, and because he loved her, he
would protect her as best he could. It was the only way he
knew to love. For Sam and Dedrah and Heather he
would do the same, and so it was no real effort to tell
himself that he went now to Layne for their sake. It was
the only acceptable reason for which he could go. Seeing
her would bring both pleasure and pain for him, but he
would see her, and he suspected he would even be glad for
the pain because it was the only way to have the pleasure. One day, when Sam and Dedrah were married, he
would no longer have an acceptable excuse—one day
much too soon.

Chapter Eight

He was undeniably angry, but she had known he would be. Proud men did not take well to being manipulated or fooled, and because he was proud, she wished she could have found another way, but she hadn't. Sighing, she sat down and prepared to endure a fit of temper, but he merely stood in the center of the room, head bowed over the hat in his hands, a muscle working in the hollow of his jaw. After a very long while, he lifted his head to look at her.

"It can't make any difference, you know," he said softly. "I appreciate the trouble you've gone to, getting me here, having Sam and Dedrah leave me by taking off in *my* truck..." He turned with a half step and waved a hand in the direction of the laden table. "Bringing in all this food." He bowed his head again, and when he spoke next, his voice was husky and thick and full of regret. "But it can't make any difference. If I allow it to make any difference, you will be hurt, and I simply can't have that."

"*This* is hurting me, Rod," she exclaimed, coming out of her chair. "I don't care about petty gossip, I care about you!"

He shook his head. "You wouldn't call it 'petty' if you knew what it was really like."

"But I do know! I heard what you heard that night, remember? I was as appalled as you, and as hurt."

"I'm sorry," he said gently, grimacing, "but I don't think that's possible. It wasn't you they were denigrating, but if we keep seeing each other, it will be. That's why we can't go on as before. Surely you see that."

"But I don't!" she cried. "All I see is that you're letting a few gossipmongers keep us apart!"

"Letting?" He erupted, truly angry now. "Do you think for one minute that if I could control it, I'd have it this way? Like you, I don't have a choice!"

She thrust her fist into her mouth to keep from screaming in frustration. Why wouldn't he listen? Was there nothing she could say to make him understand? Perhaps words would not communicate how much she missed him, how much she wanted and needed to be with him. Perhaps action was necessary. She pushed her arms down rigidly at her sides and stiffened her spine. Like a soldier marching into battle, she crossed the room.

"I don't care what anyone says about us," she told him fervently, gazing up into eyes more blue than she'd remembered. "I only care that there is an *us*." With that she lifted her arms about his neck and went up on tiptoe to get at his mouth, maneuvering around the hat held in front of him. To her absolute delight, he tossed away the treasured hat, and his arms came around her in the same smooth movement, tightening until she was pressed along his entire length, the air crushed out of her lungs. And oh, his mouth! It was as if his whole being were concentrated there in his mouth, and he was giving it to her, joining it to hers.

Then, gradually, the kiss became something more, something primitive and elemental. What had begun as a gentle but intense melding became a tangle of lips, tongues and teeth as she sought to communicate and fill needs. She wanted to sink roots into him, to attach him to herself, to bind him so that nothing could separate them—not his good intentions, not gossip, not mistakes, not even divergent desires. As their mouths blended and clashed and blended again, Layne felt that she could defeat any of those threats. She tried to tell him that she wanted him more than anything else on earth— with the body she pressed to his, with hands that took desperate hold of anything they could find and a mouth both giving and taking. If he was not participating as wholly as she, if there was reluctance in him, if his kiss felt fraught with the bittersweetness of parting and regret, it was only because she had not effectively communicated her message, and to prove it she redoubled her efforts, only to feel him pulling inexorably away.

Determinedly, he broke apart their mouths and briefly pushed her away. Then he hugged her close, her head tucked beneath his chin. It was then that she really knew what was happening. She was making a fool of herself. She wrenched away, crying out her anguish, watching as it ripped cruelly along his nerve endings. When she had stopped it with fiercely clamped jaws and a hand slapped over her mouth, he seemed to let go of the air in his lungs and calm himself before prodding his big, solid body into movement. He walked across the room, slowly bent, and picked up his hat, his face a study in control. He placed the hat upon his head, tugged it into the preferred place and smoothed the brim into perfect shape.

"I'm sorry," he said lightly. "It is all my fault. I should never have begun with you."

"No, you shouldn't have," she said, trembling and choking with the effort, "if you're going to let something so petty come between us."

"It's not petty to me," he rebutted softly. "You can't understand that, and I hope you never will, but if you come to, it won't be because of me."

"And I hate you for that!" she snapped unthinkingly.

He winced and nodded and turned away.

"Oh, Rod, I didn't mean that!" she cried, running after him.

His head jerked around. "Mean it!" he ordered savagely. "Mean it, and welcome to it!" Then he swept through the door, slamming it behind him. For once he did not remind her to lock it. It was well and truly over then. He had withdrawn even his protection.

Layne stared at the unlocked door, then numbly she turned away, and her wide, lost gaze fell on the table laden with untouched dishes of food. Nothing! She had accomplished nothing with all this pain, not even a decision on the reception menu. She started to laugh at that. For once she had not thought of business first, and once again, it seemed to be all she had, all that mattered. She laughed until tears filled her eyes; then she sat down on the floor and let them fall.

Nothing had been decided about the menu for the reception, and of course, Rod would not come to her. Neither, she knew from painful experience, would he accept her telephone calls, and when she had called Dedrah, the girl had responded almost angrily that she didn't want to even think about the planned wedding. Apparently she and Sam were fighting. It was as if all their lives were suddenly falling apart, and Layne felt helpless to do anything about it.

The days after the disastrous sample buffet were empty and leaden, but at least they were busy. What had happened that night was never far from her thoughts, and in quieter moments, she relived it over and over—every word, every gesture, every expression and especially the kiss. She had made a fool of herself with that kiss, but it seemed to her, after bitter reflection, that it was not the first time. Had he ever been as enthusiastic in that area as she had? Certainly he had never seemed in danger of losing control when kissing her, whatever he might have said. She began to fear that she would drown in despair. Going through the motions helped, so she gave herself up to her business—the one solid thing in a suddenly ambivalent life. And it was business that sent her once more to Rod Corley.

A decision had to be made on the Corley/March reception menu, providing the wedding was still on, and Layne no longer felt her clients trusted her judgment. Communication was necessary, but the telephone had proven unreliable. This would have to be handled in person. It took several days to pluck up her courage sufficiently, but finally she was in the car driving the six or seven miles into the countryside toward Rod's ranch. Despite her best intentions, a kind of apprehensive hope, heavily laced with anticipation, replaced the despair blanketing her.

She had never been to Rod's place, but both Rod and Dedrah had offered descriptions during conversation, and Layne knew enough about the surrounding countryside to know where to find the ranch house. The name on the mailbox assured her that she had, indeed, found the right place, and she turned across the cattle guard and into the long drive with a sense of accomplishment added to her jumbled feelings. The drive was a single lane of oiled and packed dirt across a pasture of sown fodder. A number of cattle with coats of brick red, black, white or some combination thereof, plodded toward a block of salt and a vertical feeder recently stocked with broken bales of sweet-smelling hay. Apparently it was feeding time on the Corley ranch, and Layne hoped that Rod was not out in some distant pasture tending his herd.

She need not have worried, for when she gained the timberline the scraggly post oaks parted to reveal the ranch house tucked in among them, and Rod's truck was parked beyond it at the side of a large blue sheet metal barn. The house was neither as small and shabby as Rod had described it nor as fine and spacious as Dedrah's description. It was, instead, a neat frame house with white siding and a blue shingle roof, a small front porch and a large rock chimney. One portion of the house was two-story, but Layne knew that the second floor contained only two bedrooms and a small bath, while the larger downstairs portion contained the family room, kitchen and dining area, a third bedroom and a second bath. In Layne's considered opinion, the house would look very pretty with shutters and flower boxes to dress the windows and shrubs to hide the foundation. A porch swing and a few potted plants would be nice, as well.

Layne parked the car and turned her attention toward the barn, from which Rod was striding. He wore a battered felt cowboy hat, faded, soiled jeans, rough boots, the top of a set of insulated underwear, leather gloves and a heavy flannel shirt, open but with the collar turned up against the chill breeze. As he walked, his strides long, determined, agitated, he stripped the thick gloves from his hands and tucked them into his back pocket. He didn't stop until he reached the passenger door of her car, which he unceremoniously jerked open. Accompanied by the sharp cold and the musty aroma of hay, he slid inside, snapping the door closed against the chill.

"H—hello," she said uncertainly.

Some unidentifiable emotion flashed over his face, to be replaced almost instantly by a scowl. "You shouldn't have come here," he said, glancing in the direction of the barn door, where a couple of obviously curious men lazed.

She felt a sharp stab of disappointment, not in the least diminished simply because she had expected that he would not welcome her. His attitude made her feel as if he was ashamed to be seen with her in front of his hired help. Reflexively, she lifted her chin. "I had no other choice. You wouldn't have taken my calls."

"There's no reason why I should," he told her tersely.

"I don't happen to agree with you," she retorted, angrier and more bitter than she had imagined, "but then I'm not the coward you are."

Anger glazed his eyes an icy blue. "If you had any idea what you were talking about—" he began.

She cut him off cold. "Let's not go through *that* again. I'm just here to do what you pay me for."

"Oh?"

She ignored the skepticism in his voice. "You may recall that I had planned a buffet of sample dishes for the wedding reception, but somehow we never got to it. So now we have to go through the ordeal again, and soon. I *must* have your decision on the menu as quickly as possible."

He grimaced and waved a hand dismissively. "I don't know the first thing about reception menus. Make the decisions yourself." He sighed, sounding abruptly tired. "No one really gives a flip anyway," he grumbled.

Irritation flared into pain, as a scab picked at until it erupts with blood. She knew her tongue was going to run away with her even before she opened her mouth, but she could no more stop herself from speaking than she could stop the beat of her heart. "Then why are you doing this!" she demanded, every word shrill with censure.

"You know perfectly well why!" he snapped.

"They don't want your wedding!" she cried. "And why should they? Who in their position would want to make such a spectacle of themselves? If you cared half as much for Sammy and Dedrah as you do for the poor, maligned Corley name, you'd allow them what they really want!" She stopped, realizing that he had gone ashen, dismay flooding his gaze with wounded vulnerability.

"And what," he said in a rough, strangled voice, "would that be?"

She almost reached out a hand to him, knowing she had hurt him. Sammy was right. He cared deeply, wanted only the best for them. It had been cruel to tell him how they despised his efforts on their behalf. Why hadn't she bitten her tongue? She could think of nothing that would help now, no way to take back the truth. It seemed that the only thing she could do was to answer his question. She steeled herself mentally, carefully choosing her words.

"A wedding," she began softly, "is meant to be a joyous affair. It should be a celebration of the union of two hearts, planned and executed by two people who want to share their love with friends and family. That's all Sam and Dedrah want, Rod—a celebration rather than a spectacle.''

He turned his head and stared out the window, hands splayed upon his thighs. His fingertips trembled. Layne felt tears pooling in her eyes. As if he, too, felt those tears, he suddenly spoke.

''Corleys don't have such weddings,'' he said, the wistfulness of his tone failing utterly to mask its bitterness. ''Not yet,'' he went on, ''but maybe someday. Maybe Heather's children will outlive the Corley reputation. Maybe her grandchildren will know joyous weddings.'' He turned his head then to look at her. ''If we're careful,'' he said urgently, ''if we plan right, step right, handle ourselves in just the right manner, if we give them something else to remember, then maybe people will forget. Sam and Dedrah understand, and that's why they're willing to go along with my plans!''

''No!'' she exclaimed. ''That's not it at all! Sam and Dedrah have gone along with this lunacy simply because they *love you,* not because they care about your precious Corley reputation! No one cares about that but you, and your obsession with it is cheating them out of their happiness, not to mention cheating me of mine!'' Again, her mouth had overrun her best intentions, but she was beyond caring just then. Not even the horrified look on his face diverted the wave of despair that engulfed her. Suddenly she could not bear a moment more of his company and the pain it brought. Lunging sideways, she leaned across him, found the door handle and yanked it, pushing the door open with her fingertips. ''Get out!'' she ordered, swiping at the tears that spilled over her cheeks. ''I mean it. Get out! Get out!'' She pushed against his shoulder, moving him not an inch but making her point well enough to get him moving on his own.

He crawled out of the car, his long frame doubled up so that he could look back in at her. "I'm sorry," he said. "If I could only make you understand—"

"I understand only too well!" she flung at him. "I understand that you think this obsession of yours gives you the right to order other people's lives! I understand that love is just not enough for you, and that's sad, Rod. It's so very sad, because it means you'll always be trying to live down shame that isn't even yours!"

The look on his face was absolutely bleak, as if she'd just given him a glimpse of a cold, certain future, but then the old familiar determination set in. She saw all too clearly now how it was with him. He had dealt with the situation in one way for so long that it had become almost a mantra, a defense mechanism to keep the old pain at bay. He *couldn't* let go. His determination to face down the gossips was all that stood between him and the raw pain of shame. Amazing. And hopeless. She grabbed the key and wrenched it to the right, grinding the starter in her eagerness to get away. He straightened and pushed the door closed. She turned the car and headed it home as fast as she dared without once looking back.

Why was she such a fool? Had she really hoped he would be glad to see her? And how could she have told him how Sam and Dedrah felt about his wedding plans for them? She pounded the steering wheel in frustration and remorse, determined never to make this mistake again.

When the reverend walked into her shop and smiled down at her, she was not surprised. She had not expected Bolton Charles exactly, but considering what she had said to Rod Corley the day before, she had known someone would come. She did not expect that person to be happy with her. She had, after all, spilled the beans, so to speak. She had told Rod what Sammy and, by default, Dedrah had been determined *not* to tell him all along, that his grandiose wedding plans were unwelcome and unwanted, even resented.

Thinking back to her actions the day before, made her miserable, a state of mind her expression must have clearly conveyed, for the Reverend Bolton Charles bent and patted her hand where it rested in her lap.

"There, there," he said kindly, "it isn't that bad."

"But I told him," she protested softly, and the reverend nodded his head in understanding.

"In my opinion, he needed to be told," Bolton said, "though it was not my place—or yours—to tell him."

"I didn't mean to," she whispered piteously. "I was angry. I was hurt. It just fell out of my mouth. I didn't even realize what I'd done until later."

"No one's blaming you," Bolton told her. "Both Sam and Dedrah understood at once how it must have been. I think in a way they are both relieved. However, the situation is rather strained, and for that reason they have asked me to speak to Rod on their behalf, to try to make him understand that, though they love and respect him and realize he is only doing what he thinks best, they want to marry in their own way and are willing to live with the consequences of doing so."

Layne sighed dramatically. "This is all my fault. I'm to blame for this."

Bolton chuckled and pulled a chair out from the table to sit down. "As best as I can make out, Rod's father and Sam's are to blame for this mess. From what Sam has told me, neither was, shall we say, the wholesome sort."

"I'm afraid he's right," she confirmed. "It's as if what they were and what they did so colored Rod's life that he still can't escape the shame he felt because of them."

"It's not an uncommon situation," Bolton told her. "Perhaps it's hard for those of us who were blessed with stable, loving homes to understand, but I fear that for all too many in this society it is the norm. The real surprise," he went on, "is that Rod has somehow beaten the odds and become a responsible, caring human being when his prime examples ought more likely to have led him in the opposite direction."

"Oh, he's responsible all right," Layne quipped. "Too responsible. As far as he's concerned he's responsible for the lives of everyone around him, but it's true that he's caring, too. He may be the most caring man I've ever known, and that's saying something." She bit her lip and glanced down at her hands, the sadness and feelings of loss sweeping over her again. With effort, she managed to brighten after a moment. "If anyone can reach him," she said softly, "it's you, Bolton, if only because you have in common with him that great capacity for caring."

"Don't credit me with too much, my girl," he warned gently. "At any rate, it is not in my hands, but God's."

She nodded. "Aren't we all?"

"Indeed, as my wife is so fond of telling me."

To her shame, Layne realized that she had not asked about Carol, whose problems were so much greater than her own. She rectified that oversight immediately, then had cause to regret it.

"The prognosis is not good," Bolton told her, his voice calm but laden with emotion. "We had hoped, at the least, to halt the spread of the cancer, but so far we have been unsuccessful."

"Oh, Bolton, how awful!" she exclaimed, fresh tears suddenly dangling upon her eyelashes.

"Now, now, none of that," he said, patting her hand again. "She would be most upset to see your tears. I honestly believe it is the sadness of others she finds most difficult to bear. She says, in fact, that she could leave this world happily, knowing heaven as her destination, if only we would let her go in like manner."

"But how can we?" Layne asked, and he gathered her hands into his, squeezing gently.

"We can't," he said. "That's just the problem, but I've come to understand this much, Layne. Our tears are ultimately for ourselves, for the loss we dread to come. How can they be otherwise when we know what awaits Carol? Heaven was made for such as her, I'm certain of it."

She nodded her agreement. "Everyone who knows Carol knows what a pure heart she has, what a clean soul."

"So," he said strongly, "as our tears are for ourselves, let us save them, for her sake, until we've actually suffered the loss."

"What a wise, compassionate man you are," she said, pulling her hands away to wipe the tears, "and how good of you to take on Sam and Dedrah's problems at such a time as this."

"I welcome them," he told her. "Helps me keep my mind off my own problems."

"Then I'm glad for all concerned," she replied, sniffing, "because I know that if anyone can reach Rod, you can."

"God willing," he said, getting to his feet. "I'll let you know how I fare."

"Thank you."

He smiled and departed, his demeanor that of a man confident in all things. She envied him that, envied him his acceptance of all things, his certainty that his God was in control at all times. How many of the world's seekers ever achieved that level of peace in faith? Too few, she decided, too pitifully few, and she was definitely *not* one of them. The proof of that lay in the uneasiness with which she passed the afternoon. It was, unfortunately, justified, and she knew it the instant Bolton Charles returned, by the look on his face.

"Rod Corley is a stubborn man," he said. "I'm sorry but he's hurt right now. Maybe we can talk again later."

Her disappointment was palpable. It weighed on her like an anvil—great, immutable, impervious. "I can't say I'm surprised, knowing Rod."

Bolton shook his head. "Stubborn doesn't begin to describe that man. Actually, he ended the confrontation by pointing out, rightly so, that I am not a parent."

Layne gasped. "Oh, Bolton, I'm so sorry. He didn't know what he was saying."

"I know. It's all right. My only concern is for Sam and Dedrah."

"Do you think they'll go through with the wedding, then?"

Bolton shrugged. "I can't say, but I'm going to advise against it. I may not be a parent, but I still don't see that I can do otherwise. They should've married long ago, or at least it seems so to me, not that I can even advise them or do anything else without their permission."

"Perhaps not," Layne said, a new idea entering her thoughts, "but I can."

"Do you want to explain that?" Bolton asked, but she shook her head.

"Let's just say, Reverend, that I've decided to take a leaf from Rod Corley's book. He's not the only one who can live by his convictions, however painful it might be."

"Always an honorable intent," Bolton muttered. "You'll call me if you need me?"

She smiled, feeling the clouds of depression lift slightly for the first time in many days. "Of course," she said, "if you'll promise to do likewise."

His answer was a clasp of her hand.

After he left for the second time, Layne called and canceled an appointment, rescheduling it for the following day. Next, she instructed Frankie and Angie to field any unexpected calls and arranged for one of them to remain later than usual. Then she got in the car and headed out to Rod's.

It was late when he heard the car, the short winter day having settled into another long, empty night. His dinner was on the table, but he got up and headed toward the door, reaching it just as the first knock came. He opened up and found Layne on his front porch, shivering inside her coat. Seconds passed before he thought to flick on the porch light. She appeared angry, almost belligerent, and seeing her that way pricked his own temper.

"I see Charles has reported back," he commented caustically.

She ignored the gibe, stuffed her hands into her pockets and squared her shoulders. "I came to tell you something. I resign. I quit. I'm no longer your wedding consultant. Of course, the arrangements I've already made stand, and you're free to go on from here—if you can—but I will no longer be a part of forcing those two kids to go through an elaborate spectacle they do not want, merely for the sake of your pride."

He gaped at her. "My pride!" How dare she blame him? Didn't she know that he was suffering, too? He said the first hurtful thing that came to mind. "Is it my pride that is the problem, Layne, or are you just looking for a way to end your association with the Corley name? I knew you'd come to it sooner or later."

She actually smiled, then shook her head. "Boy, when you're wrong, you're really wrong," she said calmly. "I wanted so much to go on with you. I even imagined myself in love and dared to envision a future, but you just couldn't let it happen. I've finally come to realize that all you really care about is what others say about you, when all that truly counts is what you *are*. Unfortunately, you aren't what I believed you to be, and I'm sad for you because of it. So very sad."

"Are you through?" he asked bitterly. The wounds were so many and so deep that he almost expected blood. She had loved him. She had dreamed of a future with him, a future that could never be. He wanted only a quiet corner now where he could suffer in silence.

She cocked her head to the side. "Be careful, Rod," she said gently. "Be careful or you'll lose us all."

He stared at her a moment through the yellow light of the porch lamp, then he lifted a hand and passed it over his eyes and through his hair. "I didn't want to lose any of you," he said roughly. "But maybe it's for the best."

"How can you believe that?" she asked, her voice little more than a whisper.

He didn't answer. He simply had to believe it. How could he go on otherwise? But then, did he even want to go on now? Why should he? For so long, Sam had been his only reason for going on, then for a while, he had had Layne. He watched longingly as she turned away and walked slowly into the darkness. Suddenly, like Sam, she was gone, and he hadn't quite figured out how it had happened. He loved them. Oh, how he loved them! And he wanted to protect them. Was his protection really worse than the danger from which he wanted to save them? God help him if that was so. God help him even if it wasn't, for now he had no one else. No one. He had wound up exactly as he'd always known he would—alone, so very alone.

Chapter Nine

Layne reached out a hand to each of them. "I'm so glad to see you."

Sammy bowed his head, suddenly shy, and Dedrah sent him a look of loving concern. "We wanted to ask you in person," he said.

She smiled. "Ask away."

"Will you come see us married on Saturday?"

"It's at the church, you know," Dedrah put in. "Reverend Charles is going to do it about eleven in the morning."

"Just family and a few friends," Sammy said. "No reception or anything like that. Just a simple little service."

"And we were hoping we could still get the dress," Dedrah said. "I was thinking we could cut it off just at the knee, you know, and leave off some of the embellishments."

"I think we can manage that," Layne told her happily. "It's paid for, after all."

"And you'll come?" Sammy asked again.

She laid a hand upon his shoulder. "It will be my pleasure, Sam, a genuine honor. Thank you for including me, especially considering that I was the one who shot off her mouth."

"Hey, we're glad you did," he told her, "except..."

"Except Rod won't be there," Dedrah continued. "I mean, there's no reason to go on with what he had you planning. He's not even insisting that we do, but he won't come to see us married our way, either."

"I hate that," Sammy said. "I know he's hurt, but he won't let me make it up to him. He just said it was better for everyone if he stayed away, something about secrets better kept. Then he warned me that everyone would know I got Dedrah pregnant and no one would give us a chance. A chance for what? We just want to be together, and I'm sorry if he can't understand that. It makes me feel bad."

"Oh, I'm sure he does understand, Sam," Layne told him. "It's just... I don't know. He's still trying to protect you."

"From what?" Sammy demanded.

"From..." Should she tell him the truth? No. Of course not. It wasn't her place. But shouldn't he know the truth about his own parents? Yes, just not from her. She swallowed what she was tempted to say and shrugged. "Life, I suppose," she finished weakly.

"But that's impossible!" Sam exclaimed.

"Yeah, but I know how he feels," Dedrah admitted. "I'd keep life from hurting Heather if I could."

"I know," Sam said. "It's just that I'm worried about Rod. He's so alone, you know, and it doesn't have to be that way. Family ought to be able to disagree without it affecting the way they feel about one another. Well, I'm not gonna let it affect the way I feel about him, and I'm going to keep inviting him to our wedding—and I won't stop asking him until it's time to leave for the church!''

"Maybe he'll change his mind," Layne said hopefully, but she had to wonder. That stubborn, stubborn man. He had only been doing what he thought best, but now that his plans were thwarted, why couldn't he unbend just a little bit? Sammy was his nephew, the boy he'd raised to a man, as much a son as any born to him could be. Shouldn't that mean more than a difference in opinion? Shouldn't it transcend the petty, malicious gossip of a few unkind, unprincipled people? Despite everything, she hadn't expected this of Rod. He cared. She knew he cared. He wanted to give these two so much and was withholding the very thing they wanted most— himself. It was perverse. The man was perverse. She prayed he would show up at that church on Saturday morning—for his own sake as well as for Sam's and Dedrah's.

He wasn't there when Bolton looked at his watch and calmly pronounced, "Time."

Sam and Dedrah stood with hands clasped, staring out into the street. Dedrah looked very pretty in her simple, knee-length dress. A little pillbox with a big bow and a wisp of veil covered the crown of her head, her hair dark and shiny beneath it. She wore pearl studs at her earlobes and a single strand around her slender neck. Sam looked quite handsome in his new black double-breasted suit and retro print tie. Heather was dressed in strawberry velvet, her skirt standing out straight over layers of baby-size petticoats and white tights with a ruffled seat.

She was adorable, her little bottom bobbing down from beneath her hem with every awkward, shaky, assisted step. She seemed determined to walk, though it was quite early and her little legs bowed precariously beneath her weight. Dedrah's parents each took one tiny hand and patiently led her into the chapel. Only then did Dedrah cast a regretful look over her shoulder.

Reluctantly, Sammy gave up the vigil. He dropped his bride-to-be's hand and slipped his arm about her waist, gently turning her toward the door. "It's time," he said, "past time. Let's do it."

Dedrah nodded, a dim smile upon her lips. Together they walked through the foyer and into the chapel. Reverend Bolton Charles followed. Layne lingered a moment longer, watching as the sun split the gray, leaden sky and spread crystal brightness over the church yard. It was as if God smiled down on this place, blessing the union that was about to be made. She wished fervently that Rod was there to see it, but he wasn't. She turned away and slipped into the chapel.

Only about ten people were present, one of them a young man in a military uniform who performed the function of best man, a role Rod could have played if he hadn't been so stubborn. The maid of honor was a cousin of Dedrah's. Carol Charles sat in the far right corner of the front right pew, looking pale and thin, a grayish cast to her once glowing skin. Her smile was serene and gentle, her hands folded in her lap. The reverend had already taken his place before the altar, a Bible open in his hands. Sam and Dedrah stood side by side facing him, and he began.

"God in his wisdom and goodness has ordained marriage for the benefit of man and woman . . ."

Layne sat in the back and listened to the words of the simple ceremony, her spirits lifting somewhat as the rightness of this union came to her. These two loved each other, and that love made them unafraid to face the world with their hopes and dreams—and mistakes—pinned to their chests. She envied them. She envied them so very much, and she wished Rod could see them now, standing together so proudly, pledging themselves before God and man, so sure, so strong. Sam's voice, clear and level, repeated the vows spoken first by Reverend Charles. Then Dedrah softly but surely followed. The reverend paused for prayer, seeking God's blessings upon this union, then pronounced them husband and wife, smiled benignly as they kissed and presented them to the small assembly as Mr. and Mrs. Samuel Corley.

A murmur of congratulations went around, growing louder and more distinct by increments. Bolton took the license from his coat pocket, unfolded it and spread it out upon the altar, then offered a pen to the bride and groom and the two official witnesses. He added his own name last to the document. When all the signatures were completed, he folded the paper once more and put it back into his pocket. Later he would affix the proper seal and mail it off. In a few weeks, the state would mail it back to Sam and Dedrah, duly stamped and recorded. She didn't imagine it would make them grin any wider than they were doing just then.

They lingered inside a few minutes longer, but there was no reason to stay. It was done. They were married. She heard Sammy say that he was going to take his wife and daughter to lunch. His soldier friend swore that Sam had been too nervous to eat a bite of breakfast, and Sam admitted sheepishly that it was so. Everyone laughed. Then Sam shook Bolton's hand and slipped him a folded bill in payment for services rendered. Layne knew full well that the money would find its way into some pocket other than Bolton's. He preferred to live on his salary, donating the little extras that came his way to any number of worthy causes. Most often, it went into the benevolent fund.

Finally, Sam took his daughter in hand, smooched her chubby cheeks and carried her out into the crisp sunshine, his wife at his side. The whole gathering followed. Rod Corley stood on the sidewalk, his hat in his hand.

He looked devilishly handsome in his dark blue suit and pale gray shirt, a burgundy-and-gray tie knotted neatly at his throat. He toyed with the hat, running his fingers around the inside of the crown, eyes darting away and back again every few seconds. Layne's heart turned over in her chest. It was enough for her that he'd put in an appearance at all. She longed to run to him and throw her arms about his wide shoulders, but she dared not. He wasn't here for her. That was over, and his family needed, wanted him.

She hung back and watched as Sam passed his daughter to his wife, whispered something into her ear, and walked over to his uncle. The two men rocked back on their heels, speaking in low, terse tones. Then Rod's hand came out, and Sammy's grasped it, and suddenly they were embracing, their hands clasped between them.

Laughter bubbled up from Layne's throat. A smiling Dedrah carried Heather forward, and as soon as she was within grabbing distance, the little one lunged out and was swept up into her uncle Rod's arms. He kissed her, then Dedrah put her arms about his waist and squeezed him. Layne was so happy for a moment that she was dizzy. Dedrah stepped away, taking Heather back onto her hip, and Rod's gaze turned in Layne's direction.

Her heart was suddenly in her throat. She held her breath, waiting for him to come to her. If only he'd take that first step in her direction, she'd fly to him. If only... But he turned away and began to fit his hat onto his head. She clamped her teeth onto her bottom lip, biting back a gasp of disappointment, and closed her eyes to the sight of him. It was Bolton's hand that squeezed her shoulder.

"Your face tells it all, you know," he said quietly. "Go on over there and say something."

She shook her head. "This is Sam and Dedrah's day. He's here for them."

"And praise God for it," Bolton acknowledged, "but I saw that look he gave you, the longing in it."

She lifted her gaze, murdering her lower lip. "Do you think so? Really?"

Bolton took her by the shoulders and shook her gently. "Love is too precious to lose, my girl. I know, because I'm losing my own. Day by day she's slipping farther and farther away from me, and there's nothing I can do but pray and trust. I don't have to tell you, do I, that I'd try anything to keep her with me."

Layne's gaze sought out Carol, so pale and wan and frail. It was as if Carol had already started to pass into that other world layer by layer. One day she would simply vanish, and this side of heaven would be that much poorer for it. Layne's gaze went back to Rod, who stood with his back to her, speaking now with Dedrah's parents and the young soldier. He was such a substantial man, so solid and human and alive. And she loved him. No use in denying that. She swallowed and licked her lips, then with a final look to Bolton for encouragement, she stepped out into the sunshine.

He knew the moment she moved toward him. Some part of him, some innate sense he hadn't even known he possessed kept him constantly aware of her. The first time she'd driven out to the ranch, he'd been in the barn helping his two hired hands load a huge round bale of hay onto a flat trailer, and the moment he'd heard the sound of a car, he'd known somehow that it was Layne's. It had been the same the second time. He'd been making his dinner and listening to the early edition of the national news. Every nerve ending in his body had suddenly come to rapt attention. He'd known who he would find standing on his porch, and in that instant he had felt all his best intentions fleeing. Then she had resigned and saved him from himself, but oh, how it had hurt.

He turned as she approached, absorbing the sight of her slender figure buttoned into a chic coat. Her hair gleamed in the sunshine like highly polished rosewood. Her face was utterly perfect, from hairline to chin, its focal point a pair of large, almond-shaped eyes so arresting a shade of green that a man felt compelled to take a second look each and every time he glimpsed them. He tried to keep the longing out of his expression as she drew nearer, but it was difficult. His feelings were all a muddle because of the situation with Sam and Dedrah. He was still uncertain about what they'd done here today, but he'd realized the foolishness of letting it stand between him and them. They were family, after all, while Layne . . . Layne was just a wish that couldn't come true. Ah, but what a wish.

She stopped not two feet away from him and turned up her perfect face, so solemn this day. He hunched his shoulders and thrust his hands into his coat pockets to counter the urge to hug her. Her lips quirked as if she knew what impulses he was fighting, and she tossed her head, sending her hair sliding back from her face.

"Rod," she said.

"Layne."

"I'm glad to see you here."

"I'm glad to see you, too. That is, I've been wanting to... apologize for wasting your time."

She looked puzzled and abruptly wary. "Come again."

He realized suddenly what she must be thinking, that he viewed the time they'd spent together as a waste, and nothing could be further from the truth. But he couldn't very well say that, so he just plowed on doggedly. "I know," he continued, keeping his voice neutral, "that you spent a great many hours on a wedding that nobody wanted and is never going to take place, more hours than you normally would have because of the short time schedule. Anyway, since you were doing it for... that is, as a favor, I figure I owe you, so I'll be sending you a check."

"That isn't necessary."

"I want to be sure your expenses are covered."

"Someone once told me that money was no object," she reminded him.

"It still isn't."

She looked away, changing the subject. "I meant it when I said I was glad to see you here. I was afraid you wouldn't put in an appearance, and it meant so much to Sam and Dedrah."

He nodded, pushing his gaze away from her. "I couldn't stay away," he said, frowning at the gruffness of his voice.

"Do you still think it was a mistake," she asked, "them marrying like this?"

He sighed. "I don't know. I think it's the hard way to do things, but it's obviously the way they want to do it, and my staying away wouldn't have served any purpose. I mean, they're going to need me."

"Yes, they are," she agreed. Then, to his amazement, she gently said, "I need you, Rod."

Heat swept through him, starting at his face and rushing downward to explode in his groin. She needed him—like she needed pneumonia. He closed his eyes, breathing deeply in an attempt to clear his head. "You don't know what you're saying," he finally managed.

She laughed, a husky, mirthless chuckle. "You know, everyone but you considers me a pretty smart woman. I'm a college graduate. I've built a successful business all by myself. I own my own home. My friends like me. My family is proud of me. Everyone thinks I'm smart enough to live my own life and make my own decisions—but you. Doesn't it make you wonder?"

"W-wonder what?"

"If maybe, just maybe, you aren't wrong."

Trapped. Neatly, unerringly trapped. He lifted a hand to his temple, smiling. "I never said you were stupid."

"The question is whether or not you think I'm smart."

"There is *no* question about your intellect, Layne."

"Then why won't you believe that I know what I'm doing? Why won't you believe me when I tell you that I don't care what anyone says about you or your family or me or anything that pertains to you and me?"

"I do believe you," he answered softly.

"But?" she prodded, fixing him with a narrow gaze.

"But I think you could change your mind," he told her honestly. "I think it's an uninformed decision. I think you've never entered a room and heard whispers run around it. I think you've never been snubbed in public by someone you thought was a friend. I think you've never seen the damage a particularly vicious rumor can cause. Most of all, I think you don't deserve that kind of treatment and shouldn't be subjected to it."

"And I think you're overprotective, controlling and paranoid!" she fired back, and when he opened his mouth to protest, she held up a hand, forestalling him. "You don't know everything there is to know about me, hotshot. For one thing, only last year a particular client of mine started a nasty little rumor about me. It seems that her daughter was left waiting at the altar and somehow it was all my fault. According to her, I so mishandled all the arrangements that I drove the lot of them to distraction, and because the poor groom just couldn't take it, he split two hours before the service. People were actually buying it, too, until it came out that he had absconded with one of the bridesmaids, whom he promptly wed in Texas."

"That's hardly the same thing," he said, but she rocketed on.

"I've heard over and over again through the years that I do what I do because I myself was left at the altar, though how that is supposed to create a preoccupation with weddings, I don't know. Some people still believe that I take kickbacks from all my sources, and one woman informed me that she knew for a fact my markup on garments was over a thousand percent! Another fruitcake told the whole blasted town that I stole one of her dress designs! It was a dress I'd made from a published pattern! Now tell me again that I've made an uninformed decision."

He shook his head. "I'm sorry people spread those rumors about you," he said, "but you could always deny them because they weren't true. That's a luxury I don't have."

She screwed her face up, twisting about irritably. "All right, your father was a criminal. Your brother was a bounder. I have a crazy aunt in North Carolina who hasn't taken a bath in forty years! None of that has anything to do with us! I'm clean. You're a decent, honorable man whose major fault happens to be a stubborn streak a mile wide. Get over it already because I'm running out of patience! I won't always be here, Corley, waiting for you to decide that the past and a few wagging tongues aren't going to run your life.''

She put her hands to her hips and waited for a reply, but for the first time he didn't know what to say to her. She had neatly poked holes in every argument that came to mind. And yet, she couldn't honestly want to share with him the Corley reputation. Could she? No, of course not. Still, it wasn't *his* reputation that was the problem, really.

Those who actually knew him trusted and respected him, the people with whom he did business, the people he called friends. At least he had come to believe that was so, until he'd heard those two talking the night of the Cattleman's Ball, then suddenly it had been as if he was right back where he had started, trying to live down the legacy left him by his father and older brother. Suddenly it had seemed that everyone who saw him was thinking about the past, his dubious heritage, but was that really so? Layne said it was only a few out of a whole town of good, reasonable people. Should those few be allowed to influence his life? Or was he just trying to justify letting this lovely woman share his disgrace?

He shook his head, unaware that his expression was an eloquent statement of the confusion and doubt he was feeling. ''I—I don't know what's best right now. I only know that I have to do the right thing for you.''

To his surprise, a smile curled her mouth. ''If you want to do something right and good for me, Rod,'' she said quietly, "come to dinner at my place tonight. That would be right for me, for us."

"'Dinner,'" he echoed, and she laughed.

"Yeah, you know, one of those three squares you're supposed to get a day."

Dinner or anything with Layne sounded absolutely wonderful, but he wasn't sure he should go. He only knew that if he did go to dinner with her, he'd better be willing to go the rest of the way, because there would be no going back once he got started on that path again. He didn't have the strength to hurt her twice. She seemed to realize he didn't have an answer for her. She turned aside suddenly, and her gaze seemed to go to Rev. Bolton Charles and his wife.

"Did you know Carol might be dying?"

He felt as if he'd been struck, his eyes instantly targeting the Charleses. "Oh, no."

"It's tough to think about. We went to school together. Did you know that?"

He shook his head. "What's wrong with her?"

"Cancer. They wanted to have children. Apparently, she thought she was pregnant, but it turned out to be cancer." She hunched her shoulders as if a chill wind had kissed the back of her neck, though the day remained calm and bright. "I feel so sorry for Bolton. He loves her very much."

"I think I owe the reverend an apology," Rod whispered.

She turned to face him. "It seems a shame to me to waste love when others are losing theirs. And it's out of their hands. God isn't giving them any options."

He understood what she was telling him. The Charleses didn't have any choice, but he and Layne did. His choice. But what if he made the wrong one? What if he decided that she knew very well what she was getting into, only to find later that they were both wrong?

"I have some thinking to do," he said to no one in particular.

Layne bowed her head, then lifted it again. "Well, you think all you want, Rod," she said. "I'll have dinner ready about eight o'clock, and you can join me or not. Your choice."

His choice again. He watched her walk away, speak to Sam and Dedrah and head for her car. Dinner at eight, and dinner would be the least of it, if he could convince himself that this lovely, loving woman belonged with him, a Corley. He pulled his hands out of his pockets, intending to cross the yard to Rev. Bolton Charles, but before he'd taken two steps, Sam called out to him and was jogging his way.

"Hey, Rod, want to have lunch with us?"

Rod laughed. It seemed everybody wanted to feed him today. It'd be nice to have lunch with his family, now that they all really were family. But his gaze crept back to the good reverend. He had some thinking to do, decisions to make, and something told him Bolton Charles could help. In addition to that, he really did owe the reverend an apology. He shook his head.

"Sorry, Sam. I need a word with Reverend Charles. Besides, I'd think you'd want to have your family all to yourself today."

Sam clapped Rod's shoulder with his hand. "You are my family, Rod. That's something I'm pretty proud of, by the way."

Rod smiled. "Thanks, son."

"There's nothing to thank me for," Sam said. "I'm the one who should be thanking you. You've given me so much, Rod. I must seem awful ungrateful turning down that big, fancy wedding you wanted for us.''

''No, I never thought of it like that.''

''Good. I'm glad to hear it.''

''We do need to talk, though, Sam. Soon.''

''Sure. What about?''

Rod steeled himself. He didn't want to do this. Dear God, he didn't want to do this, but if he didn't, someone else would, what with all the talk that was bound to be going around. He took a deep breath. ''We need to talk about your parents, Sam.''

''You're my parent, Rod,'' Sam told him softly.

''Oh, son.'' Rod put his arms around the boy. No, not a boy, not for a long time now. ''Thanks, but, Sam, there are things you don't know, things I never wanted you to know.'' His voice broke.

Sam squeezed him and stepped back. ''Whatever it is, it doesn't matter,'' he said.

''I hope you can still say that after we talk,'' Rod told him.

Sam smiled. ''I will. Come on over later. About six?'' He started backing away. ''Gotta go, man. The *wife* is waiting.''

Rod laughed. He wanted to be happy for them. ''That little woman's got a ring in your nose already,'' he teased.

''And how!'' Sam admitted. ''It's not half bad. You ought to try it.''

''Don't think just because you're a married man you can start giving me advice.''

''That'll be the day!'' Sam said loudly.

A day not too far distant, Rod thought. He waved goodbye and turned toward the church. Most of those present at the wedding had already gone, but Dedrah's bridesmaid and her mother were chatting up the reverend. Fortunately, they moved away just about the time Rod got there.

"Hello, Rod," Bolton Charles greeted him. "Nice to see you again."

"You're a generous man, *padré,* if you can say that after our last meeting."

Charles shrugged. "We had a difference of opinion. No big deal."

Rod nodded. "If you say so. Still, I feel I owe you an apology. That crack I made about you not being qualified to advise me because you aren't a parent. That was . . . cruel. I'm sorry."

Bolton pursed his mouth in understanding. "Layne told you about my wife."

Rod swallowed. "Yes. I'm very sorry. If there's anything I can do . . ."

Bolton surprised him with a smile. "You owe me no apologies, sir, and your prayers would be appreciated."

"There must be something else," Rod persisted. "I understand ministers don't make much money, so if you'd allow me . . ."

The reverend raised both hands, shaking his head. "No, no, that isn't necessary. We're well insured." He laughed then. "Layne certainly has you pegged."

"Oh? How so?"

"She told me not too long ago that you are a generous, caring man—who feels responsible for the lives of everyone he meets."

"You sure the word she used wasn't *controlling?*" Rod said cryptically.

Bolton chuckled. "Not that I recall."

"Well, I recall."

Bolton's fine black brows rose. "Tell me," he said, "what are you going to do about her?"

"I don't know." Rod sighed. "I just don't know."

The reverend nodded sagely. "It's true that I have no practical experience as a parent," he said, "but love is something I *do* know about firsthand. Will you let me give you a piece of advice in that area?"

"I was hoping you would."

Bolton nodded. "You just tried to give me money, Rod, and I'm touched, but if there's one thing that my situation has taught me, it's that the only thing of real value any of us has to give is our love. I think that's the truth God would have me learn from this tragedy of Carol's and mine."

"But to learn it at such cost!" Rod countered.

"Yes, I quite agree. On the other hand, who can know the mind of God, question His reasons?" He smiled to himself. "Do you know what my wife thinks about it? She thinks it is a truth God has given me to make it easier for me to go on with my life, to ensure that I will give my love again after..." He cleared his throat. "Forgive me. I'm emotional today. Performing this wedding has reminded me once again how much I have to lose. Carol would say how much God has blessed me. She's a re-remarkable woman, you know, a special woman."

A special woman, indeed. Remarkable, indeed. A woman who could face death with such wisdom and bravery and generosity of spirit that she could tell her husband that God would have him love again. Now that was love. That was the kind of love Layne deserved. But could he, Rod Corley, give it to her? Could he not? He looked at Carol Charles, saw her smile and wondered at it. Surely her God could give him his truth, too.

"Excuse me, Reverend," Rod said. "I have some thinking to do."

"You might try a little praying to go along with it," the reverend advised gently.

Rod nodded. "Yes, sir," he said. Thinking and praying, that was exactly what he had to do, and a lot of both.

Chapter Ten

For Layne the afternoon crept by second by interminable second. Mrs. Stapleton and Leslie came in with a retinue of female relatives and friends to see Leslie's wedding dress.

"You don't mind, do you, Miss Harington? We just couldn't wait until the wedding to show it off."

She did mind, intensely. Her thoughts simply were not on business, and complicating matters was the fact that the shop always had a good many drop-ins on Saturdays. And Leslie was unpleasant at best, not exactly endearing herself to Layne or her employees. Nevertheless, Layne put on her best wedding consultant's face, smiled serenely and offered Mrs. Stapleton's guests coffee before escorting a smirking Leslie into the dressing room.

The enormous, ornate ball gown with every furbelow and accent imaginable was brought out, divested of its tissue and plastic cocoon, pressed lightly and lowered over Leslie's swollen head. Clearly the girl was entranced, but she made a show of tugging and frowning and criticizing little details. She then pranced around in front of the mirror for a full quarter hour, pulling her hair up with her hands, pushing it forward on her head, scooping it back. After that she demanded a brush from her purse in order to repair the damage she had done to herself. Finally, she was ready to show off for her mother's party. Thirty minutes of gushing compliments later, she was ready to be assisted out of the garment.

Unfortunately, that was not the end of the visit. Leslie took so long to put herself back together that Mrs. Stapleton decided to go over the wedding dossier with her company. They picked over every detail, undoing several in the process, and one of them managed to spill a cup of coffee on the sample books, ruining several fabric swatches. Layne kept her temper only by leaving the room and dispatching Frankie to handle the cleanup. She wanted desperately to walk out of the shop, go home and dig in the garden, an illogical pursuit given the season. Instead, she made a note to order another sample book first thing Monday morning. It would cost a pretty penny, but she had every intention of seeing that the Stapletons paid.

The remainder of her business day was equally busy, so busy it bordered on chaos, and still time seemed to drag by. Uppermost in her mind was the question, *Would he come?* She knew she would be devastated if he did not. Everything rode on this dinner. If he came, they had a chance. If he didn't, then obviously he could not be moved from his position.

She had thought that she was resigned to the idea that it was over between them. Now she knew better. Somehow hope had managed to live in her heart, and only today had she known it, but everything she was and everything she felt told her tonight was make-it-or-break-it-time. Consequently, she was anxious for the evening to come yet morbidly dreaded its coming. Neither circumstance lent itself to the swift passage of time, and so she waited, or rather, endured.

When at long last she was able to close up shop and escape, she made a dash to the supermarket, picking up garlic bread, pasta and the ingredients for a good marinara sauce. She already had the makings of a fine salad at home in the refrigerator. After much deliberation, she chose a frozen apple pie for dessert, wishing she had time to make her grandmother's renowned chocolate apple cake instead.

At home, she hastily did some straightening up before jumping into the shower. Then it was into the kitchen to slide the pie into the oven and put on the marinara sauce, first sautéing chopped onion and garlic in a combination of margarine and olive oil, then adding canned tomatoes, tomato paste and fresh herbs, thyme, parsley and oregano. With that on to simmer over a low fire, she rushed back to the bedroom to blow-dry her hair, slap on light makeup and agonize over what to wear. Before she could decide, it was time to put on the water for the spaghetti. She raced back to the kitchen, filled her largest pot with enough water to get the job done, coated the top with olive oil and set it to heating over a high flame.

Back in her bedroom again, she tore through her closet with a vengeance, coming at last to settle upon a pair of soft mustard-colored slacks and a matching turtleneck sweater. Looking at herself in the mirror, she decided the outfit needed dressing up. She tried scarves, necklaces, belts and cardigans. Finally choosing a gold chain link belt hung with replicas of old coins, she looped it about her waist and secured it loosely, allowing it to ride against the tops of her hips. A pair of dangly matching earrings had come with it, but she had never worn them, considering them too flamboyant for the shop. Tonight, however, they felt appropriate. She parted her hair on the side and brushed it until it crackled and shined, then spritzed it lightly with hair spray before sliding the French hooks into the tiny holes in her earlobes. After darkening her lipstick and stepping into a pair of gold, glove-soft flats, she was pleased with her appearance.

The water was boiling by the time she returned to the kitchen, but she was reluctant to put on the spaghetti to cook until Rod had arrived, provided Rod did arrive. She lowered the flame and tried to concentrate on setting the table. Taking a simple white cloth from the linen cabinet, she spread this over the small table opposite the bar in her roomy kitchen. Next she added red-and-white-striped quilted place mats and matching napkins, then brought out her blue speckled stoneware. The result reminded her of an Independence Day celebration. The blue speckled stoneware went back into the cabinet and the black octagonal dishes came out. She found this arrangement more pleasing, especially when she added a black basket of dried flowers as a centerpiece and a pair of silver candlesticks with white candles. She brought out a bottle of blush wine and a pair of clunky wineglasses and matching water goblets. She had just finished the table setting when the oven buzzer went off. Time to take the pie out of the oven to cool and put the bread in to heat. That done, she made the salad, transferred store-bought dressing to a tiny cut-glass pitcher and filled matching bowls with Parmesan cheese and croutons.

With the salad crisping in the refrigerator, Layne looked around her and took stock. All was in readiness for Rod's arrival, but would he come? He had to. Suddenly she couldn't bear to think that he might not. She glanced at the clock—five minutes until eight. Five minutes to wait. In five minutes, she would know. After five minutes all she knew was that it was eight o'clock, the bread was ready, and so much of the water for the spaghetti had boiled away that she had to add cold water and heat up the whole pot again. Five minutes later she was pacing the floor, and ten minutes after that she was putting both the bread and the sauce pot into the oven to keep warm.

At eight-thirty, she glumly faced the fact that he was not coming; yet, she couldn't quite make herself give up. Telling herself that her appetite was gone, she wandered into the living room and picked up a novel she had been reading, but she couldn't concentrate and soon put it aside, switching on the television instead. Only when the program changed at nine o'clock did she realize that she hadn't been watching at all and switched it off again.

Numbly, she went into the bedroom and sank down onto the side of her bed. He wasn't coming. It was really over. He didn't love her.

Her chin began to wobble and tears filled her eyes. Slowly she lay back, pulled a pillow from beneath the bedspread and hugged it to her.

She had never felt so lost and alone in her life. She had offered herself in love and been rejected. No matter how noble his reasons, the sting of rejection was sharp and deep. After a long while, she had no real notion how long, she thought about how Rod must have suffered like this at various times in life. It must have hurt him badly to be equated with his father and brother and condemned out of hand, rejected, disdained. Shouldn't that have told him how she would feel at this moment? But perhaps he had realized all along that he didn't love her as she wanted, needed, to be loved. She closed her eyes, remembering how he had kissed her, the barely leashed passion against which he seemed to struggle at times, his coolness at others. She thought, too, of tenderly spoken words and small jests and the husky rattle of his chuckle, and she ached with longing and loss.

Suddenly she felt an intense desire to speak with Bolton Charles. If anyone could help her forgive and forget, it was the patient, wise minister. He would understand her jumbled feelings and help her make sense of them. He knew about love and loss. On the other hand, Bolton had his plate full at the moment with Carol fading away in illness. Her heart went out to them, but, as incongruous at it seemed, she also envied them. They shared an uncommon love. Whatever happened, whatever the future held for them, they would always have that, and it was priceless, utterly priceless. Even with his wife dead to this world, Bolton would always know that she had loved him with every fiber of her being, every stroke of her heart. He might face loss, yes, a deep, punishing loss that would throb and hurt and drain him, but never would he feel rejected, disdained, abandoned by the one he loved. Feeling that pain and even a bit of what could lay in store for Bolton, she sobbed until, at some point, she drifted into emotionally protective sleep.

When she first became aware of the ringing she felt as if she had slept for hours, buried beneath layer upon layer of black, numbing unconsciousness, but it had in fact been only minutes. Groggily she struggled up onto her elbows, identified the sound even then dying away into silence as that of her doorbell, and sat bolt upright, her heart beginning to hammer a wild tattoo. She pushed away questions and grasped at hope. It could be him. It could be Rod ringing her doorbell at—she squinted at the

clock on her bedside table—six minutes of ten. Spring-
ing up, she fisted her hands angrily, then released them
and frantically smoothed her hair. She had lost an earring and her belt was caught in the bedclothes. She jerked
off the remaining earring and the belt, then tore through
the hallway and living room as the bell rang again.

"Coming!" she called.

At the door, she paused long enough to catch her
breath, looked through the peephole, which told her
nothing, cast caution to the wind and yanked open the
door. Rod Corley was reaching once more for the doorbell.

"Layne!"

She lifted a hand to her mouth. He was here! Two
hours late! But why? If he had come only to explain once
more why she was better off without him, she'd flay him
alive with her tongue. Would she ever! At the moment,
however, she didn't trust herself to speak, so she simply
turned from the door and stalked back into the room. He
followed, closing the door softly behind him.

"Are you too angry to hear me out?" he asked.

Was she? Yes. And no. She shrugged.

He sighed. "I don't blame you if you are," he said,
"but I can't go away without trying."

She made no response to that, just walked across the
room to a chair and sank into it. He followed, halted and
looked around him uncertainly, then crossed to the sofa.

"May I?" he asked.

She condescended to give him a nod, but only one. He
sat. She leaned back and folded her arms across her
chest; they were trembling so that she feared he would
see.

He sat forward, elbows on knees, and studied his
hands. "I'm sorry about the time," he said. "I had to

talk to my nephew, and then I had some heavy-duty thinking to do.''

She stuck out her chin. "About what?"

"My life," he said, sighing. "My whole absurd life."

"What do you mean?" she asked, intrigued despite her anger.

He actually made a weak attempt at a smile. "He knew. He knew everything all along. I spent all those years protecting him from secrets he already knew." He looked at her squarely. "Do you understand what I'm saying? Sam knew. He knew he was illegitimate. He knew his father was cruel and self-centered. He knew his mother drowned herself. And he said it didn't matter because he had me. He said he wouldn't have changed that for anything." His voice was little more than a whisper at the end, and his lips trembled. He put his hand over his mouth.

Layne was on the edge of her chair. She was stunned. She was relieved. And suddenly she was angry again. All those secrets! All that agonizing and maneuvering! The wedding plans were just one example of what he had done, how far he had gone to head off gossip that could reveal secrets that were already known! All for nothing.

She brought her fists down on her knees. "Your damned obsession with the Corley reputation!" she yelled accusingly.

He shook his head. "It's not just my obsession with the Corley reputation," he said calmly. "It's my obsession with what the Corley reputation can do to the people I care about."

"And I suppose that includes me?" she snapped. It was a bitter question, and she could have bitten off her tongue. How obvious could she be? Might as well plead with him to love her.

"The people I care about, you mean?" he asked lightly.

She made no reply, not even with a bat of an eyelash.

He sighed. "You, most especially," he said. "Don't you see? It's because I care so much that I fear so much for you."

"Spare me!" She leapt to her feet. "That's all drivel, and you know it. It's just your way of gently telling me to get lost!"

"No," he said, sounding surprised, "it's my way of telling you that I love you."

Five full seconds passed before she could speak. Her heart was racing so that she could scarcely breathe. He loved her! But did that mean he'd given up trying to stay away from her, or merely that he was going to be heroically noble about doing so? She thought she'd bash in his head if it was the latter, but just in case it was she didn't want him to know how deeply he was going to hurt her. She'd gone more than the extra mile with him, baring her heart, confessing feelings no woman in her right mind would confess without some sort of declaration from him, but she did not have to visibly suffer for him. She squared her shoulders.

"So you love me, do you? Well, you have a funny way of showing it."

He leaned back as abruptly as if she'd shoved him. "Everything I've done has been for you!"

"Malarkey!"

"You can't possibly think I broke up with you for my own sake!"

"Were we going together?" she came back innocently.

That very noble exterior began to crack. He lowered his chin and swallowed hard. "You know we were."

"You never said so."

"For Pete's sake, we're not in high school! What did you want, my class ring?"

"I'd have taken a *cigar* ring and been happy to do it!"

"I would have done better than that!"

"Now *that* is news. And just when might you have honored me so, Mr. Corley? Never mind, I think I know. Provided, of course, that you'd heard nothing scandalous first, it would have been right after I'd helped you bully your nephew into going through with an elaborate farce of a wedding that served no purpose whatsoever!"

He gritted his teeth, pulling a breath through flaring nostrils, and flexed his hands upon his thighs. "One thing has nothing whatsoever to do with the other, and you know it!"

"Do I?"

He shot up to his feet, apparently having reached some limit, his hands balled into fists. "Damn it, Layne, I've done my dead-level best for all of you! I wanted to spare Sammy. That it wasn't necessary doesn't make me a bully! And didn't I back off once I knew what they really wanted?"

"What choice did you have after I resigned?" Layne exclaimed.

"For your information, I had already made up my mind to forget the whole thing!"

"The only thing you'd made up your mind to forget was me!" she cried.

Silence descended like a lead weight. Some part of her mind acknowledged that the world was full of sound. Outside, people were talking and laughing, cars were tearing over roads, clocks were ticking, dogs were barking, televisions were blaring, phones were ringing, but inside the silence was so deep that the world beyond might not have existed. Then it occurred to her that her world was here, there, in that stubborn, now angry man, and very likely she had lost him. She lifted a trembling hand to her mouth. He grimaced and sighed.

"It seemed best," he told her softly. "Don't you see, love? It seemed best for you, so I tried to forget. I broke up with you because it seemed best, and before that I tried to go slow with you because it seemed best, and I tried so hard to keep my hands off you because..." He closed his eyes. "Ah, heavens, what did I do so wrong?"

She stared at him a long minute, judging his sincerity. He opened his eyes, and they were clearly anguished. She recoiled inside, holding hope at bay. "Y-you might have asked me what I thought best," she said hesitantly. "You might have asked i-if I wanted to go slow." Should she say all that was on her mind? she wondered. But why not? What was left to lose at this point? She lifted her chin. "And you might have kept your hands to yourself a little less often! It doesn't hurt a woman to know she's desired! It doesn't hurt to let her know what you're feeling!" His mouth fell open, and she immediately began to backpedal, realizing what he must be thinking. "I—I mean, I wouldn't have let you... I told you in the very beginning that I wouldn't go to bed with you unless we...that is, before..." She shut her mouth.

He just stood there with his mouth open, then slowly he lifted a hand to her. "Come here," he said, and she felt her eyes growing large.

"Wh-what?"

"I said, 'Come here.'"

She took a step forward, and her hand rose of its own accord, but it was trembling, and she dropped it again.

He bowed his head, but when he lifted it again, he was smiling secretively. "Layne," he said, "I love you. Now come here, or I'll come and get you."

He loved her. Her chest seemed to expand almost to bursting. Her head was suddenly light. He loved her, and any moment now he'd come after her. But he didn't. He didn't have to. Her feet, it seemed, had better sense than she did, and almost before she knew what was happening they were carrying her toward him. He caught her hand and pulled her the rest of the way, his arms coming around her.

"Look at me," he commanded softly, and when she lifted her face to his, he bowed his head and kissed her.

It was a sweet kiss at first, much like the others they had shared, and then suddenly it was more, his hands sliding up her back and pressing her to him. At the same moment, his mouth parted hers, and his tongue plunged inside possessively, the force of it bending her head far back upon the slender column of her throat. Then suddenly he was sweeping her off her feet and up into his arms as if she were no bigger than Heather.

"I've been such a fool," he said, cradling her close as he dropped down onto the sofa, "but no more. I don't want to be alone, Layne, and I love you so much."

She took his face between her hands and tilted it downward. "I'm so glad to hear you say that! I love you, too." She was torn between laughing and kissing him again. She kissed him, moving her mouth over his provocatively.

He moaned encouragingly and, his left arm supporting her neck and head, ran his right hand up her leg and across her abdomen, coming to rest against her rib cage. She slipped her arms about his neck and pushed her tongue into his mouth, feeling the straight, smooth edges of his teeth and the sleekness beyond them. His hand backtracked to the hem of her sweater, slipped beneath it and journeyed upward. When his fingertips brushed the fullness of her breast, she retracted her tongue and gasped into his mouth. He took the advantage, pressing her down upon his arm, so that she reclined upon his lap, and his hand boldly cupped her breast before moving on to the other, his fingertips gently stroking the nipple so that her back arched convulsively. He bent over her, trapping his hand between their bodies, and fondled her swelling flesh, his mouth constantly plying hers, until she threw her head back, trembling and gulping air.

"Oh, my!" she gasped, and he lifted her against him again, his hand sliding around inside her sweater to her back. His mouth found the curve of her jaw and scattered kisses down the column of her throat and up again, then along her jaw to her ear.

"I suppose," he whispered, "that I'll have to save the rest until after the wedding, but I don't want to. Don't think for a moment that I want to."

She didn't hear a word after "wedding." Her eyes flew open and she went perfectly still. "W-wedding?"

"That's right."

"Sam and Dedrah have already had their wedding."

"I was talking about *our* wedding."

She came bolt upright in his lap. "*Our* wedding? As in you and me?"

He chuckled. "You have quite a grasp of personal pronouns. Naturally, I mean you and me."

Joy shot through her, followed quickly by…irritation. It was high time they got some things straight. Setting her jaw, Layne butted his shoulder with the heel of her palm. "Don't you ever *ask* before you start making decisions that involve other people?" she demanded.

He stared at her a moment, then rolled his eyes. "I did it again, didn't I? All right. Okay. I can do it properly, I swear. Just give me a moment." With that, he eased her off his lap, then leaned forward and pushed back the coffee table before sliding off the sofa onto his knees.

Layne started to laugh, her irritation melting as he maneuvered his long legs and big, booted feet to get turned around and into position. Once facing her, he reached for her hand and, cupped in his own, placed it over his heart. "Of all the ridiculous—" she began, but he placed a finger against her lips.

"I have the floor," he said, glancing down, "literally." She started to giggle. "Here now," he scolded with mock severity. "A straight face, if you please."

Hastily she schooled her expression. He cleared his throat. The hand with which he'd stilled her lips moved to caress her cheek, and suddenly the laughter died, leaving her aware of a painfully thumping heart.

"Layne Harington," he began softly, "because I love you more than I ever thought possible and because, as incredible as it seems, I believe you actually love me, will you marry me?"

She surrendered to the impulse to throw her arms about his neck and, for good measure, wrapped her legs about his waist, too. Then her mouth found his, and she gave herself up to demonstrating how very happy he had made her. He pressed her back against the sofa, and only after a long, sweet while did he lift his head again.

"I take it you accept."

She laughed and hugged him tightly. "Yes! Yes! Oh, yes!"

"Thank God!" he said. "Now if I can just get off my knees ..."

Actually, he didn't have much trouble. He got his feet beneath him, wrapped his arms around her back and stood, carrying her with him. She kissed him while he turned and dropped them both onto the sofa again.

"I do love you!" she exclaimed. "And, oh, Rod, I finally get to plan my own wedding!"

"Ah, about that," he said, kissing her forehead. "I figured, since we made all the decisions anyway, we could maybe keep the March date. I mean, if it's just a matter of reprinting the invitations...and you do have that wonderful dress. You know, the one you tried on for me that day."

She smiled at his phrasing. Sam and Dedrah had both been there, but he had known, even then, that she'd modeled that dress for him, only for him. And now she was going to wear it for him. In March. "You are brilliant," she said, rubbing her nose against his. Then she straightened. "However, there is a lot more to do than merely printing new invitations—a lot more."

He nodded, and she noted that his smoky eyes were suddenly very blue. "But not tonight," he said, his voice like velvet. "Tonight I just want to hold you."

She sighed, snuggling against him, her head upon his shoulder. A sense of well-being was filling her. Like the sun rising over the horizon, it sought out all the places of darkness and filled them with soft, glowing light. Everything was truly going to be all right now, better than all right. Sam and Dedrah were married now and making a home for their little daughter. Neither she nor Rod would ever be alone again. Where would they live? she wondered, then decided they both would be happiest at the ranch. Might she offer Sam and Dedrah her house then? She smiled to think of little Heather running around this place wreaking havoc. Would there be other little Corleys—hers and Rod's—to wreak havoc? She hoped so, but if not, she knew she would be happy with him. She belonged with him. Thank God he had seen that! But that brought up another question.

"Why?" she asked him, lifting her head. "Why did you change your mind?"

He stroked the hair back from her face, his expression grim. "It was the Charleses," he said. "Their situation made me realize that there are many things in this life from which I simply cannot protect you. Then I started to think, why should you face alone all the difficult things life could throw at you? And when I thought about all those things, well, I realized that a little gossip about matters long past wasn't so bad, after all. Then I talked to Sam, and I saw how I'd blown it all out of proportion. Of course, I had to argue with myself for a while. I can't help thinking that maybe I'm just justifying having what I want most."

"You're not!" she assured him quickly. "Truly, darling, us being together is the best thing for everyone."

"I don't care if it is or not," he told her then. "I simply couldn't waste what we have. I love you so much, and I'm so happy knowing that you love me, too. After seeing Carol Charles, after talking to Bolton, witnessing their bravery, any idea I had about nobility just fled. I don't even know the meaning of the word. I couldn't begin—" He broke off and hugged her close. "Oh, God," he said, "don't let anything ever happen to this woman. What would I do without her? How would I live alone?"

She eased herself back in his arms, her eyes filling with tears, tears of joy this time. "Not to answer for Him," she said with gentle merriment, "but I suspect you'll manage to survive any difficult times ahead just as you managed to survive those difficult times past. None of us is ever really alone, you know."

He smiled and kissed the tears from her eyes. "You're right, of course. How could I have forgotten such a basic truth?"

"We all forget from time to time," she said. "I did, just a little while ago. Tell you what, let's make a pact right now to continually remind each other that we're not alone. That seems to be what the Charleses do."

"Yes, it does," he agreed, "and this pact seems like a natural to me. I mean, sweetheart, just the fact that you love me proves there is a God!"

She laughed. "I feel the same way about you. Aren't we lucky?"

"I believe," he said, lowering his mouth to hers, "that the term is *blessed.*"

And he went on to prove to her just how blessed they were. After all, it *began* with the result; it began with a wedding, and it would shortly result in one. What greater blessing was there for two people in love?

*   *   *   *   *

HE'S MORE THAN A MAN, HE'S ONE OF OUR

MAD ABOUT MAGGIE
by Pepper Adams

All at once, Dan Lucas was a father—and a grandfather! But opening his arms to his grandson didn't guarantee that he'd find a place in his son's life. And the child's aunt, Maggie Mayhew, would do anything in her power to keep Dan out of her family. But could she keep Dan out of her heart?

Available in October from Silhouette Romance.

Fall in love with our **Fabulous Fathers!**

FF1093

Silhouette
R O M A N C E™

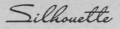

Silhouette
R O M A N C E™

The miracle of love is waiting to be discovered in Duncan, Oklahoma! Arlene James takes you there in her trilogy, THIS SIDE OF HEAVEN. Look for Book Two in October!

AN OLD-FASHIONED LOVE

Traci Temple was settling in just fine to small-town life—until she got involved with Wyatt Gilley and his two rascal sons. Though Wyatt's love was tempting, it was dangerous. Traci wasn't willing to play house without wedding vows. But how could she hope to spend her life with a man who swore never to marry again?

Available in October, only from Silhouette Romance!

Silhouette Books has done it again!

Opening night in October has never been as exciting! Come watch as the curtain rises and romance flourishes when the stars of tomorrow make their debuts today!

Revel in Jodi O'Donnell's STILL SWEET ON HIM—
Silhouette Romance #969
...as Callie Farrell's renovation of the family homestead leads her straight into the arms of teenage crush Drew Barnett!

Tingle with Carol Devine's BEAUTY AND THE BEASTMASTER—
Silhouette Desire #816
...as legal eagle Amanda Tarkington is carried off by wrestler Bram Masterson!

Thrill to Elyn Day's A BED OF ROSES—
Silhouette Special Edition #846
...as Dana Whitaker's body and soul are healed by sexy physical therapist Michael Gordon!

Believe when Kylie Brant's McLAIN'S LAW —
Silhouette Intimate Moments #528
...takes you into detective Connor McLain's life as he falls for psychic—and suspect—Michele Easton!

Catch the classics of tomorrow—*premiering* today—
only from *Silhouette*

TAKE A WALK ON THE
DARK SIDE OF LOVE WITH

October is the shivery season, when chill winds blow and shadows walk the night. Come along with us into a haunting world where love and danger go hand in hand, where passions will thrill you and dangers will chill you. Silhouette's second annual collection from the dark side of love brings you three perfectly haunting tales from three of our most bewitching authors:

Kathleen Korbel
Carla Cassidy
Lori Herter

Haunting a store near you this October.

Only from ▼ *Silhouette*® where passion lives.

Fifty red-blooded, white-hot, true-blue hunks from every
State in the Union!

Beginning in May, look for MEN MADE IN AMERICA!
Written by some of our most popular authors, these
stories feature fifty of the strongest, sexiest men, each
from a different state in the union!

Two titles available every other month at your favorite
retail outlet.

In September, look for:

DECEPTIONS by Annette Broadrick (California)
STORMWALKER by Dallas Schulze (Colorado)

In November, look for:

STRAIGHT FROM THE HEART by Barbara Delinsky
(Connecticut)
AUTHOR'S CHOICE by Elizabeth August (Delaware)

You won't be able to resist MEN MADE IN AMERICA!
